The Big Break

A Julie Classic
Volume 1

by Megan McDonald

American Girl®

Published by American Girl Publishing

All rights reserved. No part of this book may be used or reproduced in any manner whatsoever without written permission except in the case of brief quotations embodied in critical articles and reviews.

Printed in China
17 18 19 20 21 22 23 QP 11 10 9 8 7 6 5 4 3 2

All American Girl marks, BeForever™, Julie®, Julie Albright™, Ivy™, and Ivy Ling™ are trademarks of American Girl.

This book is a work of fiction. Any similarity to real persons, living or dead, is coincidental and not intended by American Girl. References to real events, people, or places are used fictitiously. Other names, characters, places, and incidents are the products of imagination.

Cover image by Michael Dwornik and Juliana Kolesova

Library of Congress Cataloging-in-Publication Data
McDonald, Megan.
The big break / by Megan McDonald.
pages cm. — (A Julie classic ; volume 1) (BeForever)
Summary: "It's 1974, and Julie Albright has just moved to a new neighborhood and started at a new school. So when she finds out the basketball team is 'boys only,' Julie is determined to fight for her right to play. Will a petition with 150 names be enough to make the coach change his mind and give her a chance?" —Provided by publisher.
ISBN 978-1-60958-451-1 (paperback) — ISBN 978-1-60958-486-3 (ebook)
[1. Women's rights—Fiction. 2. Basketball—Fiction. 3. Divorce—Fiction. 4. San Francisco (Calif.)—History—20th century—Fiction.] I. Title.
PZ7.M478419Bi 2014 [Fic]—dc23 2014019204

© 2007, 2014, 2017 American Girl. All rights reserved. Todos los derechos reservados. Tous droits réservés. All American Girl marks are trademarks of American Girl. Marcas registradas utilizadas bajo licencia. American Girl ainsi que les marques et designs y afférents appartiennent à American Girl. **MADE IN CHINA. HECHO EN CHINA. FABRIQUÉ EN CHINE.** Retain this address for future reference: American Girl, 8400 Fairway Place, Middleton, WI 53562, U.S.A. **Importado y distribuido por** A.G. México Retail, S. de R.L. de C.V., Miguel de Cervantes Saavedra No. 193 Pisos 10 y 11, Col. Granada, Delegación Miguel Hidalgo, C.P. 11520 México, D.F. Conserver ces informations pour s'y référer en cas de besoin. American Girl Canada, 8400 Fairway Place, Middleton, WI 53562, U.S.A. **Manufactured for and imported into the EU by:** Mattel Europa B.V., Gondel 1, 1186 MJ Amstelveen, Nederland.

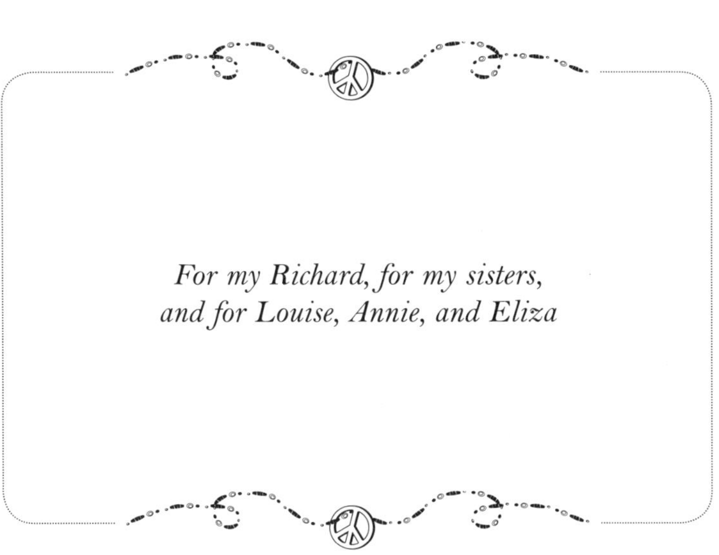

For my Richard, for my sisters,
and for Louise, Annie, and Eliza

BeForever™

The adventurous characters you'll meet in
the BeForever books will spark your curiosity
about the past, inspire you to find your voice
in the present, and excite you about your future.
You'll make friends with these girls as you share
their fun and their challenges. Like you, they are
bright and brave, imaginative and energetic,
creative and kind. Just as you are, they are
discovering what really matters: Helping others.
Being a true friend. Protecting the earth.
Standing up for what's right. Read their stories,
explore their worlds, join their adventures.
Your friendship with them will BeForever.

TABLE *of* CONTENTS

Moving Day

❁ CHAPTER 1 ❁

he world spun—first upside down, then right-side up again—as Julie Albright and her best friend, Ivy Ling, turned cartwheels around the backyard.

"Watch me do a backflip!" called Ivy. She leaned back, stretching her neck like a tree bending in the wind. Soon her shiny black ponytail bounced upside down as she twirled through the air, landing perfectly on two feet.

"I always fall flat on my face!" said Julie. "I'll never be as good as you, no matter how hard I practice." She sighed. "I'm sure going to miss doing gymnastics with you after school every day."

"I'm going to miss playing basketball in your driveway," said Ivy, "even though you always beat me."

Julie stuck out her lower lip and made an exaggerated sad face. Both girls fell down laughing. Then they stretched out on the grass, folding their hands behind their heads, and gazed dreamily at the clear blue sky, a perfect September day.

"Hey, look," said Julie, pointing to an airplane high up in the sky. "Maybe that's my dad! Hi, Dad!" The two girls whooped and yelled and waved.

Mr. Albright was a pilot. Julie always waved at every airplane she saw, imagining it might be her dad flying to some exotic, far-off country.

"What are you going to miss most?" Julie asked.

"Walking to school together and sitting behind you in class," said Ivy. "Passing notes and braiding your hair when the teacher's not looking." Julie had long, straight blond hair, and Ivy could make a teeny tiny braid down one side in seconds.

"Who am I going to be lunch buddies with?" said Julie. "You're the only friend in the world who would trade me your Twinkie for a pickle!"

"Julie!" Mom called from the back porch as she took down some hanging geraniums. "Time to get a move on. The van will be here in half an hour."

Julie and Ivy turned cartwheels all the way to the back steps. "I guess I better get going," said Ivy.

"Not yet!" said Julie. "Come up to my room with me while I make sure I'm all packed."

Upstairs, Julie scooped up Nutmeg, her pet rabbit, from her favorite spot in the laundry basket and plopped down cross-legged next to Ivy on Mom's old footlocker. It was covered with travel stickers of Big Ben, London Bridge, and the Eiffel Tower. Ivy stroked Nutmeg's velvet-brown fur, while Julie scratched her pet behind her floppy lop ears. Nutmeg snuffled softly, and her sleepy eyes started to close. "I'm sure gonna miss you, girl," said Julie, kissing her on her wiggly nose and nuzzling her whiskers. "But Ivy's going to take extra-special good care of you whenever Dad's gone."

Julie took a long last look around her room. Ghosts of posters that had once decorated the walls formed an empty gallery around the room, showing off the flowered wallpaper. Craters in the blue shag rug made a strange moonscape, a map of where Julie's desk and dresser had once been. Boxes were piled up everywhere.

"It looks like a fort in here," said Ivy.

"Remember when we built that fort out of clay we dug up from the garden? And we dressed up our Liddle Kiddles in old-timey clothes."

"I remember," sighed Ivy. The room turned middle-of-the-night quiet. Julie and Ivy couldn't look at each other.

"I still can't believe you're moving," said Ivy, flashing her dark eyes at Julie.

"It's only a few miles away, across town," said Julie. "It's not like I'm moving to Mars."

"I won't be able to blink lights at you from across the street anymore to say good night," said Ivy.

"But we can call each other up," Julie pointed out. "And you'll still see me on the weekends when I come visit my dad." There was that lump again. She felt it every time she thought of being without Dad. She thought she'd gotten used to the idea of her parents being divorced, but now that she wouldn't be living with Dad anymore, suddenly it wasn't just an idea. It was real.

"Here," said Julie. "I made us friendship bracelets. We can both wear them, and think of each other." She handed a colorful knotted bracelet to Ivy.

"Neat!" said Ivy. "And it's red and purple, my favorite colors."

"Red and purple are my favorites, too," said Julie. "Also blue, green, pink, and sometimes yellow!"

"Put it on my ankle," said Ivy, holding out her foot. "Hey, do you have a Magic Marker?"

"What for?" asked Julie, taking out a pen from her box of desk stuff.

"Give me your foot," said Ivy.

Julie held out her once-clean high-top sneaker. She had doodled all over it with markers. Ivy wrote something on the rubber tip of the toe. Julie peered at the letters: A. F. A.

"A Friend Always!" said Julie.

Julie's big sister, Tracy, poked her head into Julie's room. "Mom says to start bringing our stuff down. Set it in the front room."

"Not yet!" Julie protested. "Just a few more minutes." It was bad enough they were making her move. Now they were taking away her last moments with her best friend, too.

"Mom says *now,*" said Tracy, sounding annoyed.

Julie got up and tried lifting a too-heavy box, then

set it back down and began dragging a garbage bag across the floor instead. "Now I know why they call it Labor Day," she grumbled.

"I guess I better go, for real this time," said Ivy. Julie nodded. The two friends hooked pinkies in a secret handshake they'd had since kindergarten. Neither girl wanted to be the one to let go first.

Julie, Tracy, and Mom sat cross-legged on the floor of their new apartment, holding cardboard cartons of Chinese takeout. Mom had pushed a few moving boxes together to serve as a table, and their dinner was spread out on top of the boxes.

"It's so great here," said Tracy. "I found this cool stairway you can climb up at Farnsworth. You can see all the way to that new skyscraper that looks like a pyramid." She paused to slurp some noodles off her chopsticks. "And you should see all the groovy shops I passed along Haight Street when I went to get the takeout!"

Julie admired the way her big sister was always so confident about everything. She wished she could be certain she'd like it here.

"My favorite part is that we live above the shop now," said Mom. "Think of it! To go to work, I just have to run downstairs!"

A few months ago, Mom had opened a shop downstairs at street level, on the corner of Redbud and Frederick, with windows that faced both streets. Mom's shop was full of handmade stuff, such as purses made of worn-out blue jeans. The shop was called Gladrags. Mom had told Julie the name was from the Rod Stewart song that went *"the handbags and the gladrags . . ."* The name was Tracy's idea. She had heard the song on the radio.

"How about you, Julie?" asked Mom. "What do you think you're going to like best about living here?"

Julie glanced around the room. Tiny rainbows of color danced across the empty walls, flashing from the prism Mom had hung in the front window.

"Well, um, I especially like the dining table," Julie decided, pointing to the boxes they were eating on. Mom and Tracy laughed.

"The real dining table isn't put back together yet," said Mom. "I couldn't find the screwdriver."

"Couldn't find the hairbrush, either, huh, Mom? Have you looked in a mirror lately?" asked Tracy.

To Julie, her fifteen-year-old sister was a teenage hair freak. Tracy actually used orange-juice cans for curlers to straighten her hair! Julie looked over at her mom's tumbling brown hair, held in a sagging bun with a pair of hair sticks. "Tracy's right, Mom. You should see—you have a big giant hair bump!"

"More like a camel hump!" said Tracy. The two girls leaned back, laughing.

"Hey, what can I say?" asked Mom. "It's hard to look like Miss America on moving day." Mom's bangle bracelets jingled as she tried to pin her hair back up.

The doorbell rang, and Tracy ran to answer it. "Mom, it's some guy," she announced.

Julie looked up from her chicken chow mein. Standing in the doorway was a curious-looking man. He had a bushy red beard and wiry red hair, and he wore a patched green army jacket and a baseball cap.

"Hank!" said Mom, standing up. "C'mon in. Girls, this is Hank, a friend from the neighborhood. He was my first customer the day I opened the shop!"

"Far out," said Tracy.

"Hank, these are my girls, Tracy and Julie."

"I've heard a lot about you from your mom," said Hank. "Here." He held out a plate covered with foil. "I made you some of my famous zucchini bread, to welcome you to the neighborhood."

"Yum!" said Julie and Tracy, peering under the aluminum foil.

"Thanks," said Mom. "Can't wait to taste it. Can you stay for some tea?"

"No, I'm on my way to a big meeting about the Vet Center. But thank you." He handed Mom the foil-covered plate, tipped his cap at Tracy and Julie, and left.

"That was so nice of him," said Tracy.

Mom nodded. "Hank's a good egg." She set the plate on the kitchen counter. "Now, where were we? Let's get this footlocker into your room, Julie."

"You're going to help me fix up my room, right?" Julie asked.

"Of course, honey."

"I need curtains," said Julie. "And a lampshade for my light."

"We can make curtains," said Mom. "And decorate a lampshade. Hey, how would you like one of those fuzzy rugs in the shape of a foot?"

"Perfect!" said Julie, helping Mom clear away the leftovers.

"I volunteer to wash the dishes tonight!" said Tracy.

"There aren't any dishes," said Julie. "We ate out of the boxes."

"Exactly!" Tracy grinned. She pretended to practice tennis against the living-room wall with a fake racket—first her forehand, then her backhand. "Did you guys know that back in the olden days, before they even had rackets, people used to play tennis with their hands?"

"I had no idea," said Mom.

"I just can't wait for school. I'm going out for the tennis team. Maybe debate, too. But definitely tennis," Tracy chattered on. "Someday I want to go to France. To the French Open."

"What's that?" Julie asked.

"It's only a world-famous tennis match. Chrissie Evert won the Grand Slam there for the last two years in a row!"

"My sister's a hair freak *and* a tennis freak," Julie announced.

Tracy pretended to lob the ball right at her sister.

"Fifteen–love!" said Tracy.

"I don't see how I'm going to start a new school this week," Julie said when Mom came to tuck her in. "I don't even know where a pencil is, or my binder or anything. What if I left some of the stuff I need at Dad's? What if I get lost trying to find my classroom? What if nobody talks to me and I can't find a friend?"

"Honey, I know this is all new, and it's not going to be easy at first," Mom said, sitting down beside Julie on the bed. "But I'll take you the first day, and we'll meet your teacher and make sure you know your way around. And how could the other kids not like you?" Mom reached to hug her.

Julie squirmed away. "You don't understand."

"You know, when I was your age, Grandpa moved us to France for a year. I could barely speak French, and I was sure nobody would ever like me."

"What happened?" Julie asked.

"Well, there was this one girl in my class. She kept trying to tell me my dress was pretty, but I thought *'Ta robe est belle'* meant she wanted me to rub a bell! I finally figured out what she was saying, and we had a good laugh. Eventually, we became best friends."

"I never knew you lived in France," said Julie. "So those stickers on your old footlocker are real? You saw the Eiffel Tower in person?"

"Sure did," said Mom. "Look, I know starting over in a new place is scary. It's scary for me, too, starting a new business. But sometimes you just have to trust in yourself and take a chance." Mom kissed Julie on the top of her head and turned out the light.

Capitals and Cupcakes

✿ CHAPTER 2 ✿

On the first day of school at Jack London Elementary, Julie missed Ivy every minute of the day. She had to memorize state capitals all by herself in social studies. She had to sit alone at the lunch table, without Ivy to help make up silly names for the strange-looking food—names like Macaroni and Squeeze with Princess and the Peas. And there was nobody to laugh with her on the playground when she spotted a funny poodle wearing a tie-dyed sweater!

Every time she walked down the hall, she found herself looking over her shoulder. Principal Sanchez was all rules and no nonsense. He pointed with a pencil and warned kids to slow down or lower their voices. "Young man, tuck in your shirt!" he told a third grader. "I hope that's not gum you're chewing," he scowled at another student. "One more warning and you'll get a demerit."

Julie soon knew all about Mr. Sanchez's demerit system. Three demerits and you had to stay after school to wash blackboards or scrub desks.

Julie's teacher wrote her name in perfect cursive on the board: Ms. Hunter.

"You forgot the 'r' in Mrs.," a boy in the back row pointed out.

"It's *Ms.* Hunter," she told the class, drawing out the word "mizzz" to sound like a buzzing bee. "Not Miss. Not Mrs."

"Huh?" The students looked at each other, confused.

"Think of it like *Mr.* You call a man Mr. whether he's married or not, right?"

The class nodded silently.

"Well, Ms. is the same thing, for a woman."

"But why?" asked a bold girl named Alison. "What's wrong with Miss or Mrs.?"

"Whether or not a woman is married is her private business," Ms. Hunter explained. "Ms. works either way."

Julie carefully wrote out "Ms. Hunter" in her best cursive. She wasn't sure she understood. Would people be calling her mother Ms. Albright now?

The only kid who talked to her all day was the boy who sat next to her in class. He had a short mop of sandy hair, a spray of freckles across his nose, and a funny name that sounded like a president. Every time Ms. Hunter called him Thomas Jefferson, Julie had to hold back a giggle. "It's T. J.," the boy corrected her.

When Ms. Hunter told the class to take out their rulers, Julie didn't have one. The girls behind her whispered and twittered. Julie heard the scornful words "new girl" and "divorce." She instantly felt her cheeks get hot. How in the world could they know about that already?

"Don't mind them," whispered T. J. "Amanda, Alison, and Angela. To get into their club, your name has to start with an A."

Julie nodded. The Water Fountain Girls. She'd seen them hanging around the water fountain that morning, pointing and snickering.

T. J. handed her a ruler. "Here, you can borrow mine. I have an extra."

"Thanks," said Julie. "We just moved, and it's kind of hard to find stuff in all the boxes."

Before T. J. could reply, Ms. Hunter broke in. "Julie Albright. In my class, we don't speak when the teacher is talking."

"But I didn't have a—"

"It's okay this time. But remember, boys and girls. Any talking out of turn is a demerit."

Great, thought Julie. *First day of school and I'm already in trouble.*

Julie sat up straight and opened her math book, but she couldn't help thinking of Ivy starting fourth grade in Mr. Nader's class. At Sierra Vista, her old school, most kids couldn't wait for fourth grade. Mr. Nader let the fourth graders hatch out butterflies right in the classroom!

As Ms. Hunter wrote a metric chart on the board, Julie imagined Painted Lady butterflies flitting and floating around the classroom. She pictured one landing on the top of her teacher's poufy hair. Julie almost giggled at the thought, but she caught herself.

"Class," said Ms. Hunter, "President Ford is about to sign a bill that will soon have the whole country using the metric system. It's what the rest of the world uses. Australia and New Zealand have converted. The metric system is taking over the world, and we Americans don't want to be left behind."

Julie sighed. *Millimeters? Decimeters? What's wrong with good old inches?* she wondered as she picked up T. J.'s ruler. She felt just *inches* away from throwing up her hands in frustration. Or was it *centimeters?*

Every day after school now, Julie came home to an empty house. She was used to having Nutmeg hop right up into her lap the minute she walked through the front door. But because of the stupid no-pets rule at the new apartment, not even Nutmeg was there to greet her. Mom was always busy downstairs with customers at Gladrags, while Tracy had started staying after school for tennis practice.

Three whole days of school had passed, and Julie had settled into a routine. A boring, lonely routine. Julie picked up the newspaper and opened it to the funnies. She read *Peanuts* first, then her horoscope, just for fun. Tracy was always bugging her, saying, "You don't really believe your fortune will come true, do you?" Julie didn't, but it was interesting to think about anyway. Today, the horoscope for Taurus said:

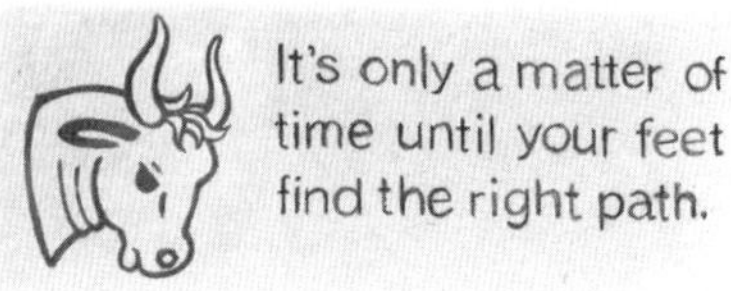

Now, what was that supposed to mean? Suddenly Julie's stomach grumbled. Maybe it meant her feet were going to find the right path to the fridge for a snack! Julie took out an orange and started peeling it.

Dense gray fog drifted past the kitchen window. Julie shivered. The house was all creepy-quiet, except for unfamiliar creaks and gurgles.

Ivy! Calling Ivy was the best cure for creepy house noises.

"Hi, Poison Ivy," said Julie.

"Hi, Alley Oop! What's up?"

"I haven't seen you for almost a week. I was wondering if you could come over this afternoon."

"You know I can't," said Ivy.

"Gymnastics?" asked Julie, but she already knew the answer.

"What else?" said Ivy.

Julie hesitated, and then asked, "Couldn't you miss gymnastics just this once?"

"I better not," said Ivy. "You know how Coach Gloria always says you don't get to be Olga Korbut and win Olympic gold medals by missing practice."

Julie wished she could go to practice with Ivy, just to have something to do and a friend to do it with. She sighed. "Oh, well, I have a test to study for anyway."

"You have tests already at your school?" asked Ivy. Julie heard a horn honking on Ivy's end. "Gotta go," Ivy said. "I'll see you Saturday. Tests—yuck!"

Julie went to her room, turned on her lava lamp, and spread out her map of the state capitals. *Tallahassee, Topeka, Trenton.* Julie started feeling cross-eyed from staring at all the names and states. She sat up on her bed and looked around her bare room.

Curtains and a fuzzy rug would be a big improvement. *Mom just hasn't had time to help me fix it up yet,* Julie reassured herself. For now, maybe it would help to at least have some of her familiar things around.

Julie opened the old footlocker. She lifted out her basketball and gave it a few friendly bounces. She unrolled the poster of Lucy, from the *Peanuts* comic, that Tracy had given her last Christmas. It showed Lucy with her fist in the air, shouting, "I'm my own person!" Julie tacked it up on her wall.

Next, she took out an envelope and peeled some of her yellow smiley-face stickers off the backing. *They should make frowny-face stickers for days like this,* she thought as she stuck them upside down onto the headboard of her bed. But even upside-down, the yellow smileys annoyed her with their cheeriness.

"Knock, knock," said Tracy, coming in through the bead curtain.

"Nobody's home," Julie answered.

"Someone's in a mood," said Tracy.

"School's hard and I have a test on state capitals and my teacher is really strict," Julie said in one big gush. "But it's not just that. I come home every day and nobody's here, not even Nutmeg. Do you know how many strange sounds a house can make?"

"You can always hang out down at the shop with Mom," Tracy pointed out.

"Mom's busy now. She has customers. She doesn't have time for us anymore."

"Of course she does," said Tracy.

"Not like before," said Julie. "We used to come home and she'd have cupcakes with gooey icing and help with our book reports and stuff."

"Tell you what. How about if I help you study for your test," said Tracy. "I'm a whiz kid when it comes to state capitals."

"I've memorized most of them, except for about twelve that I'll never get. Like Alaska. And Nebraska. And Kentucky."

"All you have to do is make up ways to remember," said Tracy. "Juneau sounds like 'Did you know?' So you think to yourself, did-you-know Juneau is the capital of Alaska?"

"Hey, that's neat!" said Julie.

"C'mon, Jules," said Tracy, standing up. "I have an idea—a place I want to show you."

A bell jingled as Tracy swung open the bakery door, and the warm air was filled with the smell of cinnamon and just-baked cookies.

"Hi, Mrs. Gibson!" Tracy waved. "This is my little

sister, Julie, and we've come for cupcakes. One dozen, please!"

Julie and Tracy oohed and ahhed and pointed through the glass to cupcakes with pink and white and lemon-yellow icing. Behind the counter, Mrs. Gibson lined them up in a box and handed the girls some tubes of colored icing.

"You get to decorate your own cupcakes here," Tracy explained.

"Cool!" said Julie. They sat down at a table in the bakery, and Tracy unfolded Julie's map of the state capitals.

"Okay," Tracy started. "There are twelve cupcakes, and twelve state capitals you can't remember, right?"

"Right. But I don't see how cupcakes are going to help me on my test."

"See, we decorate the cupcakes with a picture for each capital. When you go to take your test, you'll be able to remember the picture," said Tracy. "Here, I'll show you. Another name for hot dog is *frankfurter,* so we'll make a hot dog for Frankfort, Kentucky." She squeezed out pink icing in the shape of a hot dog. "And a little yellow icing for mustard!"

"I get it!" said Julie. "We could do a heart for Hartford, Connecticut."

"And a stovepipe hat for Lincoln, Nebraska," said Tracy.

The fog had lifted, and sun streamed through the bakery window. The bell on the front door jingled, and in walked Hank, unwrapping a scarf from around his neck and taking off his cap.

"Well, if it isn't the Bobbsey Twins," said Hank. "What are you two up to?"

"I'm helping Julie study for a test," said Tracy.

"I don't know," Hank said, stroking his bushy beard. "Doesn't look like homework to me. Julie, you're grinning like the Cheshire cat. C'mon, let me in on the joke. What's so funny?"

"I just ate Lincoln, Nebraska!" said Julie.

Jump Shots and Rebounds

❀ CHAPTER 3 ❀

he end-of-the-day school bell had rung ten minutes ago, but Julie lingered at her locker. She was in no hurry to get home to an empty house again. She closed her eyes and breathed in the familiar pencil-shaving and chalk-dust smell, and for just a moment she was back at Sierra Vista School. But when she opened her eyes, her locker stared blankly back at her. Julie pulled the most recent postcard from Dad out of her book bag and taped it to the inside of her locker door.

Just as she slammed her locker shut and started down the hallway, a ball bounced out of the gym door, off the wall, and against the lockers, and rolled down the hall, right past her feet. A basketball!

Julie scooped it up and dribbled down the hallway to the gym, glancing over her shoulder to make sure

Principal Sanchez was not nearby. A few boys were horsing around at the far end of the court, playing what looked more like dodgeball than basketball. Out of the corner of her eye, Julie saw T. J. bending down, tying his sneaker.

"Think fast!" she called, tossing the ball at T. J. He jumped up, caught the ball in midair, then drove toward the basket. Julie threw down her book bag and followed him down the court.

"Bet you can't get the ball back," T. J. teased, switching from right to left, bouncing the ball back and forth, light on his feet. Quick as a cat, Julie crouched low, sprang forward, and with one clean swipe, snatched the ball away from T. J.

"Good steal," T. J. said as Julie dribbled around him. "You shoot hoops?"

Julie did a layup, then dribbled back over to T. J. "I used to play a lot with my dad."

"Hey, how are you at jump shots? Will you try blocking me on my jump shots so I can practice? I want to play on the school team."

"There's a basketball team here?" asked Julie.

"Yeah. Fourth, fifth, and sixth graders can join.

Mr. Manley's the coach. He puts up a sign-up sheet outside his office."

T. J. turned and dribbled hard to the left, but Julie stuck to him like glue. For the next ten minutes, they took turns practicing and defending jump shots, layups, and rebounds.

"Hey, that was boss! Wanna help me again tomorrow?" T. J. asked. "Same time, same place?"

"Really? Sure! That'd be great."

"Okay. Later," said T. J.

"Later," Julie called back.

And for the first time since coming to Jack London Elementary, Julie found herself looking forward to tomorrow.

All week, Julie practiced after school with T. J. Now she'd be able to surprise Dad with some new moves on Saturday. She could hardly wait. Two whole days to see Ivy, play with Nutmeg, hang out with Dad, and sleep in her own room again. It would be just like old times.

First thing Saturday morning, Julie packed her paisley suitcase and waited by the door for Dad to arrive.

Tracy came out in orange-juice-can curlers and Miss Piggy flannel pj's, rubbing her eyes as if she had just awakened.

"You better hurry up!" Julie said. "You're not even dressed. Dad's going to be here any minute, and he doesn't like to have to wait."

"I'm not going," said Tracy.

"What do you mean you're not going? It's Saturday. It's our day to go to Dad's and spend the weekend with him."

"Well, I'm staying here. I have tennis practice anyway, and a bunch of us might go see a movie tonight."

"What about Dad? You can't decide not to go, just like that." Julie snapped her fingers. "We're still a family, you know, and Dad's part of it, too."

The orange-juice cans bounced and swung as Tracy shook her head. "Give it up, Julie. We're never going to be a regular family again. This isn't *The Brady Bunch*. Besides, I'm in high school now. I'm old enough to decide for myself what I do on the weekends."

"You think you're so—" Julie hesitated but couldn't find the right words.

Toot, toot. Dad had said he'd honk for them so he wouldn't have to find a parking place. "He's here!" said Julie. "What am I supposed to tell him?"

"Whatever you want," said Tracy. "I don't care."

Toot, toot, toot. Dad was waiting.

"So you won't care if I tell him my sister turned into an *alien?*" Julie grabbed her bag, ran down the back stairs, kissed her mom good-bye in the shop, and rushed out to the waiting car.

"You look different," Julie told Dad as she got into the car.

"Same old me," said Dad. "So, do you have everything? Where's your sister?"

"She's not coming." Julie looked down, letting her fingernail worry at a scab on her arm.

"But it's our—never mind. Wait here. I'll be right back." Dad sprinted up the steps to the front door. Julie could see him from the back, gesturing with his hands as he talked with Tracy, who stood in her bathrobe with her arms crossed. Finally, Dad came back, without Tracy, and started the car.

He was extra quiet, so Julie tried to think of things to say. She chattered on about her state capitals test, and how all the kids were looking forward to Dad coming to Career Day at school next week, and the new basket she hoped to get for her bike. It would be big enough to hold Nutmeg.

After a few blocks, Julie flipped on the radio and sat back in her seat. She made up her mind to make the most of her weekend with Dad and forget about Crabby Appleton (aka Tracy). Besides, she realized, it might be nice having Dad all to herself for a change.

As soon as they pulled up to the house, Ivy came running across the street. "Alley Oop! You're here!"

"What do you say we head down to the Wharf?" asked Dad, pulling Julie's suitcase out of the trunk. "There's a festival at Ghirardelli Square with face painting, jugglers, magicians, and even a no-hands chocolate-eating contest!"

Julie and Ivy looked at each other with delight. "Can we ride the cable car?" Julie asked.

"Why not," said Dad.

Ivy ran to ask her parents, and soon they were on their way.

Ding! Ding! rang the bell on the cable car. Julie and Ivy hopped up onto the open-air platform while

Dad paid the fare. They gripped the pole tightly, hand over hand over hand, and hung their heads out the side, where the wind whipped their hair. Wheeee! The girls giggled with roller-coaster glee as the cable car barreled down the hill toward the waterfront.

"Blue punch buggy! No punch-backs!" Julie called out, starting off the game she and Ivy played whenever they spotted a Volkswagen bug on the streets of San Francisco. She tapped Ivy on the arm, pretending to give her a punch.

Ivy scanned the cars parked along Hyde Street. "Red punch buggy convertible! I get to punch you twice! No returns!"

"Punch buggy orange!" called Dad from his seat.

"Orange?" Julie and Ivy looked at each other and laughed. "Dad, where do you see an orange VW?"

"That VW van right there," said Dad as the cable car came to a stop at an intersection. "See?" The van was covered with bumper stickers and painted daisies.

"It has to be a Volkswagen *beetle*," said Julie.

"Like Herbie, the VW beetle in the *Love Bug* movie," Ivy explained.

They hopped off the cable car near Ghirardelli Square. Music blared, kites fluttered, and a juggler on stilts amazed the crowd.

"Are those chocolate-covered apples he's juggling?" asked Ivy.

"Look," said Dad. "He's taking a bite from each apple as it goes by!"

Dad spread a blanket on the grass, and they had a picnic on the green, sipping hot chocolate as they watched a mime pretend to climb a flight of stairs.

Ivy told her friend excitedly, "Guess what! On the balance beam, we learned how to do a pike on the dismount."

Julie sighed. "That sounds really boss. I miss going to the Y after school." Then she brightened. "But I had this great idea. I'm going to play basketball. Sign-up is next week."

"That's great, honey," Dad said. "It's nice to have a club to go to after school."

"It's not just a club, Dad. It's a real basketball team, with uniforms and games against other schools and everything."

"I know you'll be a starter on the team," said Ivy.

"You're so good at basketball."

"Wow," said Dad. "They have a girls' basketball team at your new school?"

"Not a girls' team. Just a team," said Julie.

"You're joining an all-boys' basketball team?" asked Ivy.

"Why not? T. J.'s my only friend at school, and he's going to play," said Julie. "He says I'm just as good as most of the boys."

Dad put his hand on her shoulder. "Honey, I know you're good, but I've never heard of girls playing on the boys' team. It's a whole different thing playing on a team. It's not like shooting hoops with me in the driveway, or playing a pickup game at the Y. A team can be a lot of pressure."

"It's not pressure to me," said Julie. "It's fun!"

"Well, boys can be super competitive at that age, and they like to roughhouse," Dad continued. "Did you ever think they may not be too happy about having a girl on their team? I'm not so sure it's a good idea, Julie. I don't want you getting hurt."

Julie rolled her eyes. "Da-ad, I'm not going to get hurt! In the newspaper, I saw this picture of a girl from

Ohio who got to play on the boys' football team. And football's a lot rougher than basketball." She looked over at Ivy as if to say *Help me out here.*

"Yeah, Mr. Albright. Basketball's probably a lot safer than gymnastics, even," Ivy chimed in.

"Look, honey, I'm just not sure about this. Let me think about it. And I'll need to talk it over with your mother, too."

Once Julie saw the exclamation-point creases between Dad's eyebrows, she knew it was time to drop the subject.

✿

That night, when Dad came to say good night and tuck Julie in, he gave her a souvenir he had brought back from a flight to Chicago. Julie shook the snow globe. "What's this?" she asked.

"It's the Sears Tower, honey. It's brand-new, and it's the tallest building in the world. And I rode up to the top floor, one hundred ten stories!"

"Wow!" said Julie, watching as miniature snow-flakes settled around the tiny black skyscraper. What fun it would be to see real snow!

"I have a little something for your sister, too," Dad continued, holding out a tennis visor that said "Chicago" on it. "You'll take it back for me?"

"Sure," said Julie, hunkering down under the covers. "Don't worry, Dad. Mom says it's just a teenage phase."

"I hope she's right," Dad said.

Julie lifted Nutmeg up onto the bed and stroked her rabbit's ears. It felt so good to be back in her old bed. "Dad, you're still coming to school on Monday, right? Like we planned?"

"Of course. It's World's Greatest Dad Day, right? And I'm supposed to wear my pajamas."

"No, Dad! It's Career Day, remember? All the kids in my class think it's so cool that you're a pilot. You have to wear your uniform! And bring everybody those pins of wings they give out on airplanes."

"Okay," said Dad. "I guess I won't wear my pajamas, then."

"Promise?"

"Pilot's honor," said Dad. "Lights out, now. Good night, sleep tight."

"'Night, Dad." Julie waited for a moment. "Dad, you forgot—"

"Don't let the bedbugs bite!" said Dad.

As soon as the lights were out, Julie saw a flash of light in her window, coming from across the street. Ivy was signaling good night with their secret code.

Julie tiptoed across the room to the light switch. She blinked the light ten times in an on-off, on-off Morse code for *Good night, sleep tight, don't let the bedbugs bite!*

Career Day

CHAPTER 4

On Monday morning, Julie watched the clock, waiting for social studies to be over. The rest of the day would be Career Day, when some of the parents would come to tell about their jobs. Dad was going to tell an exciting story about the time he had to make an emergency landing.

The first Career Day parent was Cathy's dad, a baker who went to work in the middle of the night. He brought two boxes of cream-filled doughnuts for everybody to eat. Kenneth's dad worked at a bank and gave each of the kids a newly minted penny. Robin's dad was a dentist. He gave out special tablets to chew that turned everyone's teeth pink in the places that needed to be brushed better.

Julie was only half-listening as she toyed with her hair, trying to make a tiny braid the way Ivy used to do. It would be Dad's turn any minute. Where was he? Dad was never late—

"Sorry I'm late!" a voice whispered in her ear. Not a Dad voice. *Mom!* What was she doing here? Then, in one heart-sinking moment, Julie knew. Mom had come to break the bad news to her—Dad couldn't be here today.

"Now, our last visitor is Mr. Albright, Julie's father," Ms. Hunter announced. "Mr. Albright is a pilot."

Julie slunk down lower in her chair as Mom made her way to the front, bracelets jangling, and whispered something to the teacher. Then Mom turned and faced the class.

"Hello, fourth grade! I'm Julie's mom, Mrs. Albright. As much as Julie's dad wanted to be here, he just couldn't be. He had to fill in for another pilot who was sick. Right now he's about twenty-seven thousand feet above the Rocky Mountains."

Oh no. This wasn't happening! Julie wanted to yell STOP, but she froze in her seat while the rest of the class began firing off questions.

"What kind of plane does he fly? Is it a 747?"

"Has he ever been to Hawaii?"

"Did he ever have to make a crash landing?"

"Why is your name Mrs. Albright if you're divorced?"

The room grew quiet. The question hung in the air like fog that wouldn't lift. Julie knew it had to be one of the Water Fountain Girls who had asked it, but she didn't dare turn her head. She stared at a pair of initials carved in her desktop as if it were a work of art in a museum.

"Class," said Ms. Hunter, "remember how we talked about not asking personal questions? Julie's mother has been kind enough to take the time to tell us about her career. So let's give her our full attention. There will be time for questions at the end."

How could this be happening? Julie had bragged to the whole class about the World's Greatest Pilot, her dad. Not her mom, the . . . junk-store lady!

Mom was already pulling a heap of junk out of her old tie-dyed bag. If only Julie could be like Samantha on *Bewitched*, her favorite TV show. One twitch of the nose and she'd blink herself right out of there in an instant. While she was at it, she would blink herself back to her old school. Her old *life*.

"Have you ever wondered," asked Mom, "what to do with old string? A pair of ripped-up jeans? Even apple seeds?"

No, thought Julie. *You throw them away in the garbage!*

Mom began passing around some of the artistic handmade items she carried at the shop, like denim purses, macramé plant hangers, and apple-seed bracelets. Julie looked at the clock. Wasn't that bell *ever* going to ring?

"Did you make that neat bandanna skirt you're wearing?" asked Alison.

"What about this cool blue-jeans purse?" asked Angela, holding it up.

"I like this pink fuzzy foot rug," said Amanda. "It's so cute!"

Julie sat up straight in her chair. The Water Fountain Girls actually *liked* her mom's junk!

"Julie and I just made that for her room," said Mom.

Amanda leaned forward and smiled at Julie. "You made that?" she mouthed, opening her eyes wide and giving her the thumbs-up sign.

"Do you sell Pet Rocks?" somebody asked.

"How about mood rings?" a boy in the front row said.

Suddenly, Julie's whole class had forgotten all about pilots and 747s and crash landings. They didn't even seem to care that it wasn't a dad up there talking. They were bubbling over with questions about what it was like to have your own store.

"I want to own a pet store when I grow up," said T. J. "And have giant lizards and rare albino frogs."

"You mean anybody can just start their own store?" asked Kimberly.

"Sure," said Mom. "I'm not saying it's not hard work. Ask Julie. Some days I'm at my shop until ten o'clock at night. But it gives me a chance to do something creative, and I really like being my own boss."

Mom passed out mood rings and apple-seed bracelets to the entire class. The students immediately put them on, exclaiming, "Wow!" "Neat!" "You mean we get to keep these? For *free?*"

"It's called advertising," said Mom. "*Word-of-mouth* advertising. Maybe you'll come to shop at Gladrags now. Or tell a friend."

The whole class clapped when Mom was done. Julie glanced at her mood ring. It had changed from black to blue-green. The chart it came with said blue-green meant relaxed, calm. *Amazing,* thought Julie, realizing that was exactly how she felt.

During afternoon recess, all the kids could talk about was going to Gladrags. They crowded around Julie, asking her when the shop was open and where it was and if she could get stuff for free.

Word of mouth was . . . Julie's *mom* was the coolest parent at Career Day.

"Hey, Julie!" T. J. called, slamming his locker shut from across the hall. "Coach Manley is posting the basketball sign-up sheet after school today."

In her excitement over Career Day, Julie had forgotten that today was the day for basketball team sign-ups. She hadn't even remembered to ask Mom about it. Julie could hardly sit still, waiting for the final bell to ring. As soon as school was out, she rushed down the hall toward the coach's office.

"No running in the halls, young lady!" called Mr. Sanchez. "Even after school." Julie forced herself to slow down.

Coach Manley was a gym teacher. He had buzz-cut hair like a G.I. Joe, a growly face, and a thick neck. Every time Julie passed the gym, he was always shouting.

Julie looked for a sign-up sheet on the wall but didn't see one. She summoned her courage and knocked on the coach's door. She knew just how Dorothy felt knocking at the door of the Wizard of Oz.

"Enter," barked the coach.

Julie fixed on the bump in his nose to steady herself. He reminded her of a dragon, about to breathe fire.

"Hi, Mr. Manley," she said. "My name's Julie. Julie Albright. I'm a fourth grader, and—"

"Yeah, yeah. You looking for the sign-up sheets? Got 'em right here."

"Really? That's great! So I'm the first one?"

"Yep. How many dozen should I put you down for?" asked Coach Manley.

"Dozen? Dozen what?"

"Cookies. For the basketball bake sale," said the coach, leaning back in his chair. "We're trying to raise money for new uniforms. How about I put you down for some chocolate chip cookies. My favorite."

"Cookies? I'm not here about cookies," said Julie.

"I'm here about the team. I want to be *on* the team. The basketball team."

"We don't have a girls' team at Jack London. We can barely afford the boys' team. Why do you think we're having a bake sale?"

Julie took a deep breath. "Not the girls' team. The boys' team."

Coach Manley sat up. She had his full attention now. "Let me get this straight," he said slowly. "You want *me* to put *you* on the boys' basketball team."

Julie nodded, her heart pounding.

Coach Manley smiled and shook his head. "Young lady, the basketball team is for boys, and boys only. Got that?"

"I'm as good as the boys," Julie said softly. "Just give me a chance to try out. Please."

"Sorry. Answer's N-O, no. This is my team and I make the rules. When spring rolls around, we'll have some intramural games—softball, tetherball, badminton. Maybe you can play one of those."

Julie shook her head. "That's not the same." She flushed and looked down at the floor, embarrassed to meet his eyes. A strange new feeling washed over her. It felt like a mixture of shame, frustration, and an emotion she couldn't quite identify.

She glanced up at the coach. He had turned back to his desk, signaling that it was time for her to leave. Her instinct was to run out of his office and never see him again. But something kept her feet firmly planted to the floor.

Finally, Coach Manley looked up. "I have work to do. This conversation is finished."

Julie felt her insides go all runny, like the yellow belly of a breakfast egg. As she turned to go, hot tears smarted at the back of her eyes. Julie swallowed hard, pushing back her fear.

"If there's not a basketball team for girls at this school, you have to let a girl play on the boys' team," she told the coach, her voice shaking. "I read it in the newspaper."

"Did the paper say I don't have to do anything I don't want to do? Case closed. Out of my office."

"It's the law!" Julie whispered, backing away.

"Well, I have a news flash for you, young lady. In this gym, I'm the law." Coach Manley towered over Julie as he leaned across the desk toward her. "Now, do I have to call the principal to escort you out of here? Or will you leave on your—"

Julie didn't wait to hear the rest. She fled. She ran all the way home, wind biting her ears and stinging her cheeks.

At Gladrags, Mom and Tracy had newspaper spread across the table and counter in the back, and they were gluing beads and buttons onto blank white lampshades.

"Hi, honey," said Mom. "I was telling your sister all about Career Day. You just missed some girls from your class. I've already had three new customers since my talk today."

Julie wondered if they were the Water Fountain Girls. "That's great, Mom."

"What's wrong with you?" asked Tracy. "Your face is as red as a beet!"

"Wait!" said Julie, looking at the table where they were working. "Are these all the newspapers from last week? Thursday or Friday? I have to find something!" she said frantically, lifting up corners of the newspaper and peering at headlines. "Here it is!" She flipped the paper over to the inside of the sports section, careful to avoid getting stuck with glue, and pointed to the headline: "High School Girl Tackles Boys, School Board."

"See? This girl wasn't allowed to play on the school football team, so she went to court. She won, and they had to let her play, because of this new law."

"Oh, yeah. We learned about that in civics class," said Tracy. "They passed some big federal law to make things more equal."

"I believe it's called Title Nine," said Mom. "But what does this have to do with you, Julie?"

"It's the basketball coach at school," Julie explained. "He won't let me play on the team because I'm a girl."

"He's a male chauvinist pig," said Tracy.

"Tracy!" Mom sounded a little shocked. "Where did you hear that?"

"Some people in tennis called Bobby Riggs a male chauvinist pig because he thought Billie Jean King couldn't beat him," Tracy replied. "Then she trounced him in a big match and proved that girls can be just as good as boys in sports."

"Look, honey," said Mom, smoothing out Julie's hair. "I don't see why you shouldn't be allowed to play on the team, if that's what you really want. Let's talk this over with your dad when he gets back next week."

"I already talked to Dad about it, and even *he* doesn't want me to play on the boys' team," Julie told her. "But they don't have a girls' team. Besides, tryouts for all the positions are this week. Next week will be too late."

Julie grabbed the page with the article and rushed up to her room. She scooped up her basketball and bounced it against the wall. *Thwump! Thwump!* She knew Mom didn't like her bouncing it in the house, but the satisfying thump of the ball helped ease the bundled-up feelings inside her.

Nobody ever asked her what *she* wanted. Divorce. *Thwump.* Moving. *Thwump.* Changing schools and leaving Ivy. *Thwump-thwump-thwump!* This morning, her horoscope had said "Create your own future by taking charge." Well, taking charge was what she was *trying* to do.

Julie stopped bouncing the ball and sat up straight. She wasn't going to give up. And they couldn't make her!

Let Girls Play, Too

❀ CHAPTER 5 ❀

The rest of the week at school seemed to drag on forever. On Friday, Julie was standing in front of her locker at the end of the day when she overheard the Water Fountain Girls whispering to each other.

"Shh! There she is. She's the one," said Alison.

"The one what?" asked Angela. Or was it Amanda?

"Can you believe it?" said Alison. "She actually asked Coach Manley if she could be on the *boys'* basketball team!"

"She's a TOMBOY!" Amanda and Angela hissed, saying the word too loud on purpose.

Julie froze. She stuck her head deeper into her locker, pretending to look for her reading workbook. A voice came up behind her. "Just ignore them. You're good at basketball."

Julie pulled her head out of her locker and smiled gratefully at T. J. "Does Coach Manley already have his team picked out?" she asked.

"Nope. He's still choosing positions. I'm keeping my fingers crossed I'm a starter. Wish me luck."

"Luck," Julie said longingly, waving good-bye to T. J.

Saturday morning Julie was reading her horoscope—"Don't hesitate; today's the day to jump in"—when she heard Ivy's knock.

"You're here!" Julie said, leading her friend into the living room. The two girls pushed boxes into the corner so that Ivy could show Julie her latest floor routine.

"Did you know Olga Korbut was the first person to do a backward aerial somersault on the balance beam?" Ivy asked as she turned her handstand into a back limber.

Julie tried to copy the move, but as soon as she got into a handstand, her feet clomped to the floor.

"Girls!" called Mom. "What's going on? Sounds like a stampede of elephants in there. Julie, please tell me you're not bouncing that basketball inside."

"Don't worry, Mom," said Julie. "It's just handstands."

"Well, I don't want you two breaking your necks, either. Why don't you run down to the deli and get us some lunch meat for sandwiches, and we can have lunch in the shop. I have lots of new beads, if you'd like to make bracelets."

"Oooh, beads!" said Ivy.

"Sure, Mom," said Julie.

As the girls walked down the hill toward Haight Street, Julie told Ivy all about Coach Manley and the basketball team. "After the coach wouldn't let me on the team, Tracy called him a pig," Julie confided.

"Whoa. I'd get in big trouble if I ever called a grownup a pig," said Ivy.

"Not a *pig* pig. A *male chauvinist* pig. It's some big fancy word she learned from a tennis match. It means when boys think they're better than girls."

"I don't see why you'd want to play on a team with only creepy boys anyway," said Ivy. "They have smelly feet like pigs. Oink, oink!" Julie and Ivy pressed their noses into snouts and couldn't stop snorting and giggling.

At the corner, while they waited for the walk sign, Julie saw Hank. He was carrying a clipboard, going up to cars stopped at the light, and talking to drivers through their car windows.

"Hey," said Ivy, "let's not cross here. Let's go down to the next light."

"But the market's right there," said Julie.

"I know, but I don't think we should walk past that guy," said Ivy, pointing to Hank. "He's weird. He looks like a troll with all that orange hair."

"Oh, that's just Hank. He's a friend of my mom's. I say hi to him all the time."

"I'm not supposed to talk to any strangers," said Ivy.

"Hank's not a stranger. Besides, Mom said I should be nice to him because he's one of those guys that was in the war. A Vietnam vet," Julie explained. "She says it's really hard when you've seen so many terrible, horrible things. Some people just can't get over it."

"Well, I don't know," said Ivy.

The light changed, and Julie took Ivy's hand as they crossed the street. Ivy switched to Julie's other side so that she wouldn't have to walk by Hank. But he had already spotted Julie.

"Hey, how's Lincoln, Nebraska?" he called.

"Great," Julie called back. "I aced my test!"

"Way to go," said Hank, meeting up with Julie on the far side of the street and slapping her a high five. "Who's your sidekick?"

"This is my friend Ivy, from my old neighborhood," said Julie. "We're going to the market to get stuff for lunch. Are you coming by the shop later?"

"No, not today. Too busy." He held out his clipboard. "I still need eighty-one more signatures."

"Signatures? For what?" Julie asked.

"For my petition," said Hank.

Even Ivy was curious. "A petition?" she asked.

"We're trying to get them to open the Veterans' Center again. That's where all of us vets used to hang out. We liked to go there to chew the fat and play cards, but the center was real important. For some of the homeless guys, it was the only meal they got all day and the only place they had to clean up and stay in out of the rain."

"What happened to it?" asked Julie.

"Same ol' same ol'. Budget cuts. City said they didn't have enough money to keep it open." Hank shook his head. "But we're not giving up. If we each get a hundred fifty signatures, we can take it to the bigwigs at the next board of supervisors meeting, and they have to open the issue back up for discussion."

"I sure hope you get enough signatures," said Ivy.

"Can anybody make a petition?" asked Julie.

"Sure," said Hank. "It's a great way to get people to pay attention to your issue."

"And even if they said no about something, the petition might get them to change their minds?"

"Yep, that's what it's all about," said Hank. "Well, I gotta book," he said, tapping his clipboard. "Check you later."

"Bye, Mr. Hank!" Ivy waved.

"See you later, alligator," called Julie.

As the girls ate their sandwiches, all Julie could think about was starting her own petition. After lunch, while Ivy began stringing glass beads to make a bracelet, Julie drew columns on paper with T. J.'s ruler and numbered the lines up to one hundred fifty, just like Hank's petition.

"C'mon, Julie," said Ivy. "Don't you want to make bracelets? I'm going to make one for every day of the week!"

"Not right now," said Julie. "I'm making a petition." After all, her horoscope had said today was the day to jump in, so that's what she was doing. Julie wrote "Let Girls Play, Too" across the top of the page and drew basketballs and high-top sneakers in the margins. When she was done, she put on her roller skates.

"Hey, where are you going? I'm only up to Wednesday!" said Ivy.

"We can make bracelets any time," said Julie, waving her papers in the air. "C'mon, I need your help to get people to sign my petition."

Ivy put down her beads and trudged out the door after Julie, calling, "Wait up!"

Julie stopped at the corner. "Let's go ask that lady carrying the groceries across the street."

"For real? You're just going to walk right up to a perfect stranger and start talking to them? And tell them you want to be on a boys' basketball team?"

Julie felt her stomach do a nervous flip-flop. Maybe Ivy was right. Could she work up the courage to just walk right up to a total stranger? "Please, Ivy, just come with me."

"I don't think my parents would like me doing this," Ivy said.

Julie couldn't help wondering what her dad would say if he knew she was starting her own petition. She pushed the thought out of her mind. "Just help me get started," she pleaded. "I'll do all the talking, and if you don't like it, we can go home. I promise."

Ivy bit her lip. She did not look happy, but she followed her friend across the street.

"Excuse me," Julie called to the lady, who was putting groceries into her trunk. She held out her clipboard for the woman to see. "Would you like to sign my petition? So I can be on the basketball team at my school?"

"Sorry, not interested," said the lady, looking annoyed.

"See? What did I tell you?" Ivy mumbled.

"Let's try that man coming out of the bakery," said Julie. "Hello! Would you like to sign my petition?"

"I'm in a hurry," said the man. "Good luck."

"Boy, he didn't even give me a chance to say what

it's for!" said Julie, trying not to feel discouraged.

"How about that lady with the stroller? Maybe she likes kids," Ivy said.

Julie skated up to the lady and started off with, "Oh, what a cute baby!"

"Thanks," said the lady, beaming.

Julie held out her clipboard and explained her petition as the lady rocked the stroller back and forth.

"It's about time they started letting girls play the same sports boys get to play," said the lady. "Where do I sign?"

"Thanks a lot!" said Julie. "You're my first signature."

"I can see that. Well, best of luck to you."

"She was nice," Julie told Ivy.

"Good. Now can we go back and finish making bracelets?"

"Ivy, that's only *one* signature. I need to get a hundred fifty."

Ivy stopped. "A hundred fifty! That could take a year!"

"C'mon, it's not that bad. At least let me get a few more. Hey, there's Hank—I bet he'll sign it."

Julie skated all over the neighborhood with Ivy

trudging loyally behind. Every time the girls passed someone, Julie stopped and talked about her petition. Each time, it was like stepping out onstage at a school play, worrying she'd trip over a prop or forget her lines. But for every few people who wouldn't sign or didn't want to be bothered, Julie would find one who agreed with her.

Finally, Julie had almost one full column of signatures. She held up the clipboard triumphantly. "Look! Let's get just a few more."

"You've been saying that for hours," said Ivy. "Why can't we go back now and play Clue, or listen to Tracy's records, or do something *fun?"*

"I can't believe you think this is boring," said Julie.

"We've been doing this all afternoon," Ivy complained. "I hardly ever get to see you anymore, and I thought we were going to have *fun."*

Julie looked down at her petition. She had collected seventeen signatures, plus three blisters on her feet. She still had one hundred thirty-three more signatures to go. "Well, it's not dark yet, so I'm staying out a little longer."

"But you promised," said Ivy. "You said if I helped

you get started, we could go home."

Julie threw her hands up in exasperation. "Don't you want my petition to work? You're my best friend. Don't you care if I get to play on the team?"

Ivy shrugged. "Not if it means we have to keep doing this."

Julie spun around to face her friend. "How can you be so selfish?"

"Because you think playing basketball with a bunch of dumb old boys is more important than being friends with me!" Ivy turned and stomped off.

"Where are you going?" called Julie, skating after her.

"What do you care?" asked Ivy. Ivy's back was stiff as she stormed straight up the hill, faster than Julie could follow on skates.

"What about our sleepover?" Julie called after her. But Ivy turned the corner and disappeared from sight.

The next day, Julie woke up exhausted. Her legs ached and her head felt as heavy as a bowling ball. Her first thought was that she should be having strawberry whipped-cream waffles with her used-to-be best friend

Ivy at that very minute. Instead, she sat up in bed and blinked back hot, angry tears.

Why was Ivy being so stubborn? Why couldn't she understand? What if somebody had told *her* she couldn't do gymnastics anymore?

Suddenly, Julie felt furious—at everything. If her parents hadn't divorced, she wouldn't have had to move. If she hadn't moved, she wouldn't be going to a new school with a basketball team that didn't allow girls. She'd have spent her Saturday at the Y with Ivy instead of asking people to sign a stupid petition . . .

The petition! Julie leaped up and snatched the clipboard from her desk. She yanked out the first sheet, the one with all the signatures, and *whhht!*

She ripped the page right in half, and threw it on the floor.

Julie pulled on sweats and sneakers, grabbed her basketball, and ran outside. She dribbled—*bam bam bam*—hard and fast against the sidewalk.

"Hey, you're gonna wear a hole in the sidewalk, Sport!" called Hank, walking up Redbud Street.

Julie turned away and kept dribbling. Hank set down his coffee and bagel bag, came up behind Julie, and stole the ball right out from under her.

"Hey!" Julie chased after Hank, who dribbled down the sidewalk and juked right, then left, trying to fake her out. He spun into a driveway and lobbed up a hook shot as he passed under a rusty basketball rim attached above the garage.

"Nice shot!" said Julie, forgetting her mood. She scooped up the rebound and went for a layup herself.

"Back at you!" said Hank.

They played hoops for several minutes, until Hank flopped down on the curb. "Haven't had my coffee, or I'd be able to keep up with you," he teased.

Julie perched on her ball, catching her breath.

"So, how's the petition going, Sport? You on that basketball team yet?"

"Huh," Julie snorted. "I don't even care about that anymore. It's too hard getting signatures and they'll never let me on the team anyway and besides, I lost my best friend over it," she said in one breath.

"Oh, so you don't mind not being on the team, then?"

Julie shrugged. "Doesn't matter. It's too late, anyway. I ripped up the petition."

Hank raised his eyebrows but said nothing. He gathered up his coffee and bagel and started to leave, then turned back to Julie. "Hey, you remember President Nixon?"

"Sort of. I remember when he resigned from being president," Julie said. She also remembered her parents arguing about him, but she didn't say that.

Hank nodded. "Well, I sure wasn't his biggest fan, but I remember he once said, 'A man isn't finished when he's defeated, he's finished when he quits.'" With that, Hank turned and headed up the street.

Julie went back up to her room and stared at the torn petition. She desperately wanted to be Ivy's friend again. But what would Ivy think if she knew Julie had torn up the very signatures she had dragged Ivy along for hours to get? Maybe Hank was right. What would she gain by giving up now?

Pushing the two halves back together, Julie smoothed out her petition, then opened her desk drawer and took out some tape.

Now Julie carried the petition with her everywhere

she went. She talked to people on her way to school. She asked the teachers, librarian, and school nurse if they'd sign. And she spent every free minute after school going up and down the neighborhood, asking every person who would stop and listen to sign her petition.

But it just wasn't the same without Ivy. When a lady with a parrot on her shoulder signed the petition and the parrot mimicked, "Sign here! Sign here!" Julie knew Ivy would have split her sides laughing. And when she reached one hundred signatures, she had no best friend to jump up and down with.

The next day after school, Julie sank into a chair without even taking off her coat. She banged her clipboard down on the workroom table.

"Why the long face?" asked Mom.

"I've been out there with my petition for over an hour and not one single person would sign it today."

"Any time you try to change something, it's going to be difficult," Mom said gently. "Not everybody thinks girls should play sports. A lot of people think games like football and basketball are just for boys."

"But that's not fair," said Julie.

"I know, honey. All I'm saying is, it can take a while for people to change their thinking. There was a time, only about fifty years ago, when people didn't even think women should be allowed to vote. It took a lot of hard work for that to change."

"I know," said Julie with a sigh. She stared glumly at the floor. "I miss Ivy, though. It's not as fun without her."

"I bet she misses you, too," said Mom. "You're just going to have to give it a little time."

Thursday morning, Julie woke up early with a tingling of excitement. She dressed and ate quickly. If she hurried, she could get the last three signatures on her way to school.

Dumpsters and Hoopsters

CHAPTER 6

y the time Julie turned the corner at the bakery, she was almost running with eagerness to get to school—and Coach Manley. But she paused when she saw Hank drinking coffee through the bakery window. She walked over and pressed her clipboard up against the window. She held up one finger, then five fingers, then made a zero with her thumb and index finger. 1-5-0! Hank smiled a big grin and raised his coffee cup in a toast.

At school, Julie made a beeline for Coach Manley's office. As she cut through the quiet gym, the smell of the polished wood and the squeak of her sneakers gave her goose bumps. She pictured herself faking left, driving toward the basket, and leaping in the air to make the perfect layup.

When Julie got to his office, Coach Manley was on

the phone. She clutched the petition in her hands, waiting for the conversation to end. It was almost time for the bell to ring.

Standing in the doorway, Julie held the papers up, trying to get Coach Manley's attention. She shuffled her feet. She coughed. She was about to knock when Coach Manley motioned her in. Then he saw the papers in her hand.

"Whatever it is, Albright, just leave it," he told Julie, covering the receiver with one hand.

"But I . . . it's really—"

"I said leave it. Can't you see I'm busy right now? Stop back later."

Looking down at the rumpled, taped-together pages with curling edges full of smudged basketballs, Julie thought of all she'd been through to get those hundred and fifty signatures. She wanted to explain the significance of all those names. But she had no choice. She set the papers down on Coach Manley's desk and rushed to her classroom as the bell rang.

All day, Julie couldn't think of anything else. Finally,

in the middle of social studies, she leaned over and whispered to T. J., "Do you think Coach Manley has read my petition?"

"Julie, T. J.?" said Ms. Hunter. "Is there something you'd like to share with the class about the Mississippi River?"

"Sorry, Ms. Hunter. I—I have a stomach ache," said Julie, which wasn't exactly a lie. "May I please have a hall pass to go see the nurse?"

Julie started down the hall to the nurse's office, but she couldn't stop her feet from heading straight to the gym office. She knocked at the open door. "Excuse me, Coach Manley?"

"What is it, Albright? Shouldn't you be in class?" the coach barked.

"Did you get a chance to read my petition?" Julie asked, nervously twirling her mood ring. She was afraid to even look to see what color it was.

"I read it. Doesn't change a thing. Sports are for boys, not girls."

"But Coach, it's not just me anymore. A hundred fifty people agree that I have a right to play on the team."

"I don't care if you show me a hundred and fifty

thousand names. They're all going in the same place." Right before her eyes, he balled up the petition and went for a basket . . . in the trash can.

Julie felt as if somebody had just punched her in the stomach.

"A piece of paper's never going to get you on this team," said the coach. "Now scram, before you get a demerit for being out of class."

As Julie headed back to her classroom, trembling with anger, a voice behind her boomed, "Young lady? Are you supposed to be in the halls right now?"

Julie stopped in her tracks. She turned and found herself looking right at Mr. Sanchez's pencil, which was pointing at *her* this time. His piercing eyes made her feel like a rabbit caught in an eagle's talons.

She held up her hall pass. "I'm on my way back to class," she squeaked.

"No wandering around now. Straight back to your lessons."

"Yes, Mr. Sanchez," Julie said, hurrying—but careful not to run—back to class.

"I'm so mad, I could scream," Julie told T. J. as soon as the final bell rang. "All my hard work, and he just crunched up my petition like it was nothing but an old hamburger wrapper."

"What are you gonna do now?" asked T. J.

Julie paused. She'd been so certain her petition would work that she hadn't thought of a backup plan. There was only one thing she could think of to do. "Get my petition back."

"But how?"

"Come on. Let's go find Mr. Martin."

Mr. Martin, the janitor, was cleaning the cafeteria. He led them out the back door and gestured to seven giant bags of trash.

"They're ready for the Dumpster—but until then, they're all yours. Search away!" Mr. Martin said grandly, with a sweep of his arm.

Julie and T. J. dug right in. For twenty minutes, they were up to their elbows in milk cartons, pencil shavings, Popsicle-stick projects, and old worksheets. When Julie looked up at T. J., his face was smudged with purple from all the ditto sheets. Ordinarily, Julie knew she would have laughed to see T. J. with a purple face, but right now she was too upset.

"I don't see it anywhere," said T. J. "And I better get to practice, or *I* won't be on the team either."

"Please, T. J. Only two more bags to go. Wait! What's this? Page two—this is it!" She held up the page in triumph. It was wrinkled and smeared with what looked like chocolate-milk drips, but Julie's heart leaped. It was like seeing an old friend.

They dug deeper into the bag. "Here's another page," said T. J.

"I found page one," said Julie. "We have them all. Even though they smell like sour milk. Thanks a million, T. J."

She knew what she had to do now. It would be harder than finding her petition in the trash, harder than facing Coach Manley, harder than collecting all the signatures. Ignoring her pounding heart, Julie made herself walk down the hall to the front office. But when she got there, she froze outside the forbidding door—the door that said Joseph Sanchez, Principal.

No turning back now, Julie told herself. The flutter inside her stomach was already whipping itself up into a tornado. She summoned all her courage and knocked on the door.

"Come in," a deep voice said.

Julie stepped into the principal's office, crossing the sea of gold carpet to stand in front of his desk, which was as shiny as a polished apple. Not even one paper clip was out of place. Julie stood flagpole-straight, clutching her petition. She felt her hands grow moist. *You haven't done anything wrong,* she reminded herself.

The principal looked up from his desk. "What can I do for you, young lady?" he asked.

Julie took a deep breath and began to talk. She told him about wanting to play basketball, and how there was only a boys' team and the coach said no girls. She told him how good she was at basketball, how her father always said she could dribble like a Harlem Globetrotter, but now that her parents were, well, divorced, she couldn't play very often with her dad anymore. Then, suddenly running out of words, she handed Mr. Sanchez the wrinkled petition.

The principal looked at the first page. Julie could hear the clock ticking as he read the long list of names.

He turned to the next page, and the next. Finally, he peered over his reading glasses at Julie.

"So you're a hoopster. You know, I was a pretty good point guard myself, back in my high-school days. I used to dribble circles around some of the tallest guys on defense."

He wasn't angry with her! Julie felt herself breathe again.

"I can see this means a lot to you," Mr. Sanchez continued. "I can't make any promises, Julie. I'll have to talk this over with the school board. I'll get back to you next week."

At home that evening, Julie gushed with news of her eventful day.

"I'm proud of you, honey," said Mom, putting her arm around Julie and squeezing her tight.

"Weren't you scared talking to the principal?" asked Tracy, looking up from her homework.

"Yes," said Julie. "But he turned out to be nice. He used to play basketball, too."

Bling! The timer went off in the kitchen. Mom walked

over to the oven and pulled out a steaming casserole.

"Anyone hungry?" Mom asked. "I made tuna noodle casserole. With potato chips on top, the way you girls like it."

"You made a real dinner?" Julie and Tracy asked at the same time, looking at each other in disbelief.

"Come on, it's not all that unusual, is it?"

"Mom, we've had takeout about a hundred times since we moved," said Tracy.

"Only a hundred?" asked Julie, and everybody laughed.

"Hey, Mom, don't forget. Tell her about the thing." Tracy nodded toward the table by the front door.

The *thing*? Nervously, Julie followed her sister's glance toward the front door, but she couldn't see anything unusual.

"Oops, I almost forgot in all the excitement," said Mom. "A package came for you today."

"For me?"

"Special delivery!" Mom winked at Tracy.

The small box was taped shut and rattled a little when Julie shook it. "It doesn't say who it's from," she said, puzzled.

"Just open it!" said Tracy.

Julie ripped open the box, only to find a paper-towel tube inside with the ends taped shut. She peeled the tape off one end and shook out a rolled-up sheet of paper that fell open like a scroll.

"What does it say, Jules?" asked Tracy.

"It's a petition," Julie said slowly. "Just like the one I made for basketball, with columns and numbers and everything."

At the top were big block letters. Julie read the words aloud: "Petition to Be Julie Albright's Best Friend. One–Ivy Ling. Two–Ivy Ling. Three–Ivy Ling. Four–Ivy Ling. Five–Ivy Ling . . ."

Julie unrolled the petition all the way to the floor. "She signed it one hundred and fifty times!"

"That's some friend you've got there," said Mom.

Monday went by without a word from Mr. Sanchez. Then Tuesday. Every time Julie left her classroom, she kept an eye peeled. This time, instead of worrying that he'd point his accusing pencil in her direction, she was actually hoping to spot him, but Mr. Sanchez was nowhere to be seen. On Wednesday, Julie offered to take the roll-call sheet to the office for Ms. Hunter, just hoping that the principal might come out from behind that closed door. But he didn't.

Finally, on Thursday, shortly before the last bell was about to ring, an announcement came over the PA system. "Julie Albright, please report to the principal's office. Julie Albright."

"What'd you do?" Angela asked.

"She's in trouble!" said Alison.

It was all Julie could do not to sprint down the hall to the office. But at the same time, she could feel a knot in the pit of her stomach, a small lump of dread. What if the school board had turned her down? What if the principal had talked to her dad? What if the answer was *no?*

Mr. Sanchez was standing in the doorway to his office. "Hello, Julie," he said, motioning for her to come in and sit down. He cleared his throat. "After careful consideration, I've determined that we're not in a position to start a girls' basketball team at this time." He paused. Julie's heart sank.

"However, I've also determined that to be in full

compliance with Title Nine, our school must allow you to play on the boys' basketball team." He smiled. "So, that makes you the newest member of the Jack London Jaguars."

Julie jumped up out of her seat. She could hardly keep from throwing her arms around him. Wait till she told T. J.!

"Now, before you get too excited, I'm not finished yet. Let me stress that there may be some who will disagree with this decision, and I don't want any trouble, on or off the court. I've spoken with Coach Manley, and you will report directly to him if you have any problems."

Julie nodded. "Thank you, Principal Sanchez," she said politely. But in her mind, she was already dribbling down the hall, through the open doors of the gym, and out onto the court.

Walking home, Julie took a shortcut and realized for the first time that she knew the route by heart. She no longer had to concentrate on street names, landmarks, or left and right turns. Her feet practically bounced with the good news, past the purple iron gate, past the funny-face fire hydrant, past the giant peace-sign mural. She couldn't wait to tell Mom and Tracy, knowing how excited they'd be for her. Ivy, too.

Dad. Julie hoped he'd be happy for her. It was true that he hadn't liked the idea of her playing on a boys' team—but wasn't he the one who'd taught her how to shoot hoops in the first place?

Julie imagined bursting through the front door of their old house and announcing the good news to her whole family, all together, and then racing across the street to tell Ivy. Unfortunately, that wasn't the way it would be. But she wasn't going to let it spoil her good mood.

As Julie turned the corner onto Redbud Street, she saw the welcoming lights beneath the front awning of Gladrags, glowing as if in celebration. Mom would be there, bracelets jangling as she arranged items on a shelf or waited on a customer. And Tracy would be home any minute, tossing her tennis racket on the kitchen table, kicking off her sneakers, fixing herself a snack. In the living room, the prism hanging in the front window would just be catching the last light of day, splashing rainbows everywhere, all around the room.

Julie broke into a run, heading home.

Homework!

❀ CHAPTER 7 ❀

chool was now in full swing at Jack London Elementary, and Julie had a lot more to worry about than basketball.

Homework. She had never had so much homework before in her life! At her old school, all she'd had to do for homework was fun stuff, like reading *Charlotte's Web* or doing a word search. But Ms. Hunter's fourth-grade class had book reports to write, vocabulary words to memorize, and geography maps to draw. Julie thought she just might go cross-eyed staring at the web of pink, green, and yellow countries and continents.

And now, Ms. Hunter had just announced a new assignment—a "family project" that would stretch out over several weeks. Julie winced. Families were not Julie's favorite topic right now—not since the divorce.

Julie studied Ms. Hunter's precise penmanship on

the blackboard, trying to imitate her teacher's loopy cursive writing as she copied the topic into her own notebook:

Just then, T. J. slid a note over to her. Opening it in her lap, she sneaked a peek at it.

The Story of My Life is too much homework!

Julie looked at T. J. and grinned. Then she turned her attention back to her notebook and carefully copied the complete homework assignment from the blackboard:

My First Memory
My Brothers and Sisters
When My Mom Was My Age
When My Dad Was My Age
The Best Thing That Ever Happened to Me
The Worst Thing That Ever Happened to Me

Julie's first memory, when she was three or four, was sneaking into her parents' room and jumping on the big bed when nobody was looking. The Best Thing

That Ever Happened was easy—getting to play on the boys' basketball team. It was the Worst Thing that Julie could not imagine writing about. Julie didn't even like *thinking* about her parents' divorce.

"Class," Ms. Hunter was saying, "this project is not just for sitting at your desk and telling me what you remember. I would like all of you to be reporters here. Interview your family members and find out about them. Ask them questions. Learn something new about the people closest to you.

"I want at least one page on each of the topics," Ms. Hunter went on. "You'll also give an oral report to the class about all you've learned."

An oral report to the class! This assignment just kept getting worse. It was bad enough that Julie's parents were divorced, but did she have to tell the whole class about it?

Julie decided she would have to come down with a bad case of The Dog Ate My Homework. Or in her case, The Rabbit Ate My Homework. Maybe she'd come down with writer's cramp. Or writer's block, whatever that was. Julie pictured a gigantic toy block sitting on top of her hand, weighing it down so that she couldn't write.

When Julie went to her locker at the end of the day to grab her gym bag and head for basketball practice, she heard some of her classmates buzzing about their projects. Sure enough, it was the Water Fountain Girls, who loved to chatter and gossip.

"Oh, I can't wait to work on my family project," said Alison. "The best thing ever in my family was when we all went together on a vacation last summer to the Grand Canyon."

"I'm going to tell how my mom and dad went scuba diving for their tenth anniversary and brought back a real shark's tooth for me and my brothers," said Angela.

"My mom's an identical twin, so when my mom and dad were getting married, they played a trick on him and my dad almost married my aunt!" said Amanda. "We still tease him about how my aunt was almost my mom. I could tell that story."

Julie sighed. It was so easy for them. They all had regular families and happy, funny stories.

Maybe she could make up a pretend story about the Worst Thing That Ever Happened to her. Then she wouldn't have to write about the divorce for the whole entire class. But that would be cheating.

"Earth to Julie," T. J. said, waving his hand in front of her frowning face. "Ready for practice?"

"I was just thinking," said Julie. "About our family report."

"Don't remind me," said T. J. "What are you going to write for the Best Thing Ever?"

"Easy," said Julie. "Getting to play on the basketball team. Being one of the Jaguars is definitely the Best Thing That Ever Happened to Me."

"Speaking of basketball, you know how Coach Manley gets if we're late for practice," said T. J. "We'd better hurry, or we'll both be writing about getting kicked *off* the team for the Worst Thing That Ever Happened."

That afternoon, Dad picked Julie up after school and drove her to his house for the weekend. Funny how she thought of the house she grew up in as *Dad's* house now, Julie reflected. As they drove, Julie decided to practice for her assignment. The three best things about staying at Dad's were:

1. Shooting hoops with Dad

2. Seeing Ivy, who lived across the street

3. Playing with Nutmeg, her pet rabbit

The three worst things about staying at Dad's were:

1. Missing Mom

2. Wishing Tracy would stop being mad at Dad and join them every weekend

3. Most of her stuff was at Mom's house now.

When they arrived at Dad's, Julie headed for the back door. "I'm going to get Nutmeg."

"I already brought her in," said Dad. "She's upstairs in your room."

"Thanks, Dad," said Julie, racing up the stairs two at a time. She burst into her old bedroom and was surprised, as always, by how different it looked from before. No rolltop desk, no bookcase, no beanbag chair. This room, these four walls, this shaggy carpet were all she'd known for nine years—her whole life. But nothing felt familiar anymore. When she called softly to Nutmeg, her voice seemed to echo, bouncing back to her off the blank walls. Julie scooped up Nutmeg from her basket in the corner where the desk used to be and ran back downstairs, keeping ahead of the empty feeling that the room gave her now.

While Dad peeled an apple, Julie perched on the edge of the kitchen counter and dangled an apple peeling in front of Nutmeg's sniffing nose. Nutmeg's whiskers twitched and quivered with excitement.

"You're awfully quiet this afternoon," Dad said. "Everything okay at school? How's basketball going?"

Julie hesitated. Dad had taken the news well when she told him that she got on the boys' team. But she didn't want to tell him how the boys on the other teams sometimes called her mean names just because she was a girl. Instead, she told him about the three steals she'd made in the last game.

"Oh, man. I wish I'd been there," said Dad.

"We have a big game in two weeks, against the Wildcats, and I'm kind of nervous about it," Julie told him. "You're coming, right?"

"You bet I'll be there," said Dad.

"I also have a gigantic school project I have to start working on," Julie sighed.

"You don't sound very happy about it," said Dad.

"It's just that, well . . ." She didn't quite know how

to explain to Dad why it was hard for her to write about her family. She didn't want to make him feel bad. "It's just that—my teacher gives so much homework," Julie said finally. She described the Story-of-My-Life project and how she was supposed to interview everyone in her family.

"Sounds like fun to me," Dad said. "I think the story of Julie Albright will make a great report. You can tell about the time you tried to eat a banana slug, because you thought it was a banana."

"Da-ad! That's way too embarrassing!"

"You were only two," Dad said. "I think it's kind of cute. And funny."

"How about if I write about the time my dad fell into the duck pond at Golden Gate Park when we were playing catch?"

"Okay, okay. Truce!" Dad held up both hands palms out, as if to say *stop.*

"But I do need to interview you, okay, Dad?" Julie picked up a ketchup bottle and spoke into it. "Reporting to you live from the home of Daniel Albright, world-famous pilot. He has just returned from a daring adventure—"

"Hey, wait a second," said Dad. "Hold it right there, Ace. I have an idea." He disappeared into the back room and came out holding both hands behind his back.

"What is it?" asked Julie.

"Something I got for you in Japan. I was planning to put it away for Christmas, but it seems to me you could really use it for your school project. On the other hand, maybe we should wait," Dad teased.

"Dad! I think it's a great idea to give it to me *now!*" Julie leaped up and faked right, then left, using her fancy footwork from basketball to try to grab whatever Dad was holding behind his back.

"Time out! Foul!" Dad called, blocking Julie. "Okay, okay. I give up." Dad brought his hands out from behind his back, presenting the box he'd been hiding.

"What is it—a transistor radio?" asked Julie, looking at the picture on the front of the box. All the writing was in Japanese.

"It's a portable tape recorder," said Dad. "With a microphone and everything. It'll be great for your interviews, don't you think?" Dad pointed to the buttons. "See, if you plug in the microphone here, and put in a blank tape, you can use it to record people."

"You mean I can talk and sing into it and stuff?" asked Julie. "Then play it back and hear myself on tape?"

"Yup," said Dad.

"This is so boss! Thank you, Dad," Julie said, hugging him. "Can I go over to Ivy's and show her my new tape recorder?"

"Be back by dinner!" Dad called. Julie was already halfway out the door.

"Hey, Poison Ivy!" Julie said, bursting through the door as soon as her friend opened it.

"Alley Oopster! Or should I call you Alley Hoopster?" said Ivy.

"Look what my dad just gave me. A tape recorder!" Julie held it up.

"Far out," said Ivy, imitating teenagers they heard on TV. "Let's go to my room and try it." Ivy was sucking a grape Popsicle, and she expertly caught a juicy purple drip before it ran down her arm.

"Oooh, keep slurping your Popsicle real loud and

I'll tape it." Julie turned on the tape recorder and said, "Testing, testing, one, two, three, testing," into the microphone. Then she held it up to Ivy.

Slurp, slurp. Ivy exaggerated the slurpy-lurpy sounds.

"Louder," Julie prompted. "Now let's rewind and see if it worked." Julie played back the tape, and the two girls collapsed onto Ivy's bed, laughing.

"Is that what I sound like?" asked Julie. "My voice sounds so weird!"

"Well, don't feel bad. I sounded like a garbage disposal," said Ivy, prompting even more giggles.

"What else can we tape?" Julie asked. The girls wandered around Ivy's house, taping anything they discovered that made a noise. They taped Ivy's little sister, Missy, crying for one more cookie. They taped Ivy's brother, Andrew, snoring while he napped on the sofa. They taped Ivy's mother singing to herself in Chinese while she stirred a pot of soup on the stove.

When they played the tape back, Julie said, "Your little sister's so cute, even when she's crying."

"Yeah, but you don't get stuck babysitting her," said Ivy.

"I wish I did," said Julie. "I can't wait till I'm old enough to babysit."

"Hey, I know—let's make some sound effects," said Ivy. "Like they do in plays and movies."

"Great idea," said Julie. Putting pairs of wooden-soled clogs onto their hands, the girls clip-clopped against the floor to sound like a giant tromping down the stairs. A squeaky door sounded like a mouse when Julie held the microphone up to its hinges. For rain, they turned on the shower.

"The toilet!" said Julie. "Pretend you're about to get flushed down the toilet."

"Help!" cried Ivy. "Save me! A giant whirlpool is about to—" *Ker-plushhh!* Ivy flushed the toilet while Julie held out the microphone. They bit their lips to keep from laughing.

"Let's hear it," said Julie, hitting the rewind button. They listened to their entire collection of sound effects. When it came to the flushing toilet, Ivy said, "That sounds like Yosemite Falls!" They played it over and over, laughing harder each time.

"Hey, Ivy, I gotta go," Julie said finally. "Dad said to be home by dinnertime."

"See you later," said Ivy. "And don't forget to blink your lights tonight when you go to bed, and I'll blink mine."

"I won't forget," Julie told her friend.

Julie and Ivy played with the tape recorder all day Saturday. But after breakfast on Sunday, Julie realized that her weekend with Dad was almost over and she still hadn't interviewed him for her school project.

She popped a new blank tape into the recorder. "Go ahead, Dad, tell me a story about when you were my age."

"Let's see if I can remember that far back, to the Stone Age."

"C'mon, Dad, this is serious," Julie said.

"Okay," said Dad, settling into his favorite chair. "When I was in the fourth grade, growing up in Duluth, Minnesota, money was tight and none of us could afford a bike. So, my buddies and I fished a real junker out of the trash and fixed it all up. We painted it black and yellow and called it the Hornet. We spent a whole summer swapping that bike around. Our favorite thing was building ramps so we could do jumps. One day, just as I took the jump, my pants got snagged in the chain and I lost my balance. I went head over handlebars, landing all twisted up like a pretzel."

"Whoa! Were you hurt bad?" Julie asked.

"Well, I broke my foot, and I had to wear a clunky cast the rest of the summer. Couldn't take a bath for over a month, which I didn't much mind when I was ten, but I couldn't go swimming, either."

"Did you have to use crutches? Did it heal up okay?"

"Yup, I did get pretty fast on crutches. And the doc told me something interesting that I've never forgotten," said Dad, taking off his shoe. "In the spot where the bone was broken, it actually knits itself back together stronger than before." He took Julie's hand and ran her finger over a small bump on the top of his foot.

"That's all that's left from the break?" Julie asked.

"That's all," said Dad.

By the time Dad dropped Julie off at Mom's apartment, it was dinnertime on Sunday evening. Julie skipped up the steps to the front door, still filled with all the fun she'd had over the weekend. But when she turned to wave good-bye to Dad, she couldn't help feeling a now-familiar pang, knowing Dad was headed back, by himself, to the too-quiet house full of empty rooms.

Julie watched the beams of Dad's headlights fade as his car disappeared down the hill, and she headed inside and into the kitchen, where heavenly smells coaxed away her sad feelings.

"Hi, honey," said Mom. "How was your weekend?"

"Good. Mom, what's that great smell?"

"Just meat loaf in the oven," said Mom. "And I made gravy for the potatoes."

"It smells yummy, Mom. Hey, look what Dad brought me from Japan." Julie pulled out her tape recorder, pushed the record button, and held up the microphone.

"We're here above the famous shop Gladrags, speaking with owner Joyce Albright. Mrs. Albright, who is normally hard at work running her store, is today making a rare appearance in the kitchen. Tell us, Mrs. Albright, what's cooking for dinner?"

"I already told you it's meat loaf," said Mom.

"Well, then, what is it you're making now that's getting flour all over your apron?"

Mom dusted off her hands and brushed her apron, puffing a small cloud of fine flour in the air. "Cherry pie. All this flour is from rolling out the crust."

"Like Grandma's?" Julie asked, momentarily forgetting her reporter role. "With the fancy crust and vanilla ice cream on top?"

"That's the one," said Mom. "Julie, honey, could you put that microphone down and start setting the table? We'll be ready to eat in about ten minutes, as soon as this goes into the oven."

"Where's Tracy? It's her turn to set the table."

"Then get your sister," said Mom.

Julie set down her tape recorder, but as she started down the hall, Tracy pushed past her into the kitchen. "Mom says come set the table," Julie told her sister.

"It's not my turn to set the table," said Tracy, plucking a carrot from the salad as Mom pretend-swatted her hand.

"You're cracked. I set the table last, on Thursday, 'cause the next day I left for Dad's," Julie retorted.

"Well, I set it for the last *two* nights in a row, while

you were gone," said Tracy.

"Yeah, well, so did I, at Dad's. That's *three* nights in a row for me. But what would you know? You didn't even come to Dad's."

"Girls, girls!" said Mom. "Enough with the Hundred Years' War. Julie hasn't even been back ten minutes and you two are already at it. Tracy, get the plates and glasses. Julie, set out the silverware. You haven't seen each other all weekend, and I want us to have a nice, peaceful dinner together."

"Well, she started it," said Julie.

Mom gave Julie a sharp look. "I don't want to have to tell you again. If you two don't stop bickering, there will be no cherry pie for dessert."

"What? You made cherry pie?" asked Tracy.

"Just like Grandma's," said Julie. "With ladders for the crust and everything."

"*Lattice*," said Mom.

"Yum!" said Julie.

"That's one thing we can agree on!" Tracy grinned.

Meet Charlotte

❀ CHAPTER 8 ❀

he next day after school, the string of brass bells jingled as Julie came in through the front door of Gladrags, calling, "Hello? Anybody home?" She made her way past racks of ponchos and peasant shirts, Mexican masks and blankets, and shelves of sandalwood incense.

"Hi, honey," Mom called from the back room. "Good timing. I was just fixing myself a cup of tea. How was school today?"

"Fine, Mom. Is now a good time to tape you?"

"Sure, but if any customers come—"

Julie was already dashing upstairs. She grabbed her tape recorder and hurried back down to the shop.

Julie held out the microphone, and Mom began telling her all about the time when she was ten, growing up on an apple farm in Santa Rosa, north of San Francisco.

"I got a horse named Firefly for my tenth birthday, and of course I couldn't wait to ride her. I'd begged and pleaded for a whole year, wanting a horse of my own. But before I even climbed into the saddle, the horse got spooked and acted all crazy, rearing and jumping and bucking."

"Whoa," Julie whispered.

"She broke away from your grandpa, who was holding the reins, and ran out through the garden and around the apple orchard. We chased her for half the morning. Finally she stepped on her reins, and that stopped her."

"What spooked her so badly?" asked Julie.

"Later we discovered poor Firefly had been stung by a bee right on her nose. So I finally got my horse, but after that incident, I was afraid to ride her for the longest time."

Just as Mom was finishing her story, Tracy came in and plunked a towering armload of schoolbooks on the table. "Shh!" Julie mouthed, holding a finger to her lips and frowning.

"Is it safe to talk now?" Tracy asked impatiently when Mom finished. Julie pressed the stop button and nodded. Tracy held up a leafy green plant spilling out of a milk carton.

"What's that?" asked Julie.

"Meet Charlotte, my new roommate," Tracy said.

Mom laughed. "Your new roommate is a spider plant?"

"Oh, I get it," said Julie. "Charlotte, like the spider in *Charlotte's Web*?"

"Exactly," said Tracy.

"Who gave you a plant for a present? A boy?" Julie teased.

"No! It's not a present. It's a project we're doing in biology. All the kids in the class got their own spider plants. I have to take care of it and keep a daily journal where I track how much water it gets and stuff like that."

"That'll really brighten up your room," Mom said. "And houseplants are good to have around—they're supposed to clean up the air."

"Wow, they gave you a real live plant at school?" Julie exclaimed. "All I ever got was a potato. We made potato people in art class once."

"Well, it better not croak, because this is worth twenty points of my grade."

Julie picked up the microphone and clicked record. She pointed it at Tracy. "It helps plants grow if you play music or sing to them. Why don't you sing 'Eensy Weensy Spider' to Charlotte?"

"On tape? You have got to be kidding. I'm not singing to a plant."

"C'mon, I could use it in my family report. I have a school project, too, you know."

"Turn that thing off," Tracy said, reaching over and pressing the stop button. "Mom, do you have any pots or planters around? I have to transplant Charlotte."

"Let's see," said Mom, looking around the workroom. "Check that box on the bottom shelf."

Tracy rummaged through the box. "Hey, what's this?" she asked, holding up a clay hippo.

"Aw, that's cute," said Julie. "What is it—a candy dish with legs?"

"No, it's actually for a plant," said Mom. "A guy here in San Francisco makes them, and he gave me one as a sample, to see if I'd sell them at the shop."

"It's perfect! I bet I'll even get extra credit for having such a cute planter," Tracy crowed. "Thanks, Mom."

Julie grabbed her tape recorder and followed Tracy

up the back stairs into the kitchen.

"Stop following me with that thing," said Tracy.

"I'm not following you. I just need to tape you for school. Part of my report is about brothers and sisters. And guess what? I don't have any brothers."

"Can't you see I have more important things to worry about right now? Help me spread newspapers on the kitchen table so I can re-pot my plant."

Julie spread out the newspapers while Tracy scooped up the plant from the milk carton and transferred it into the hippo pot. She poured the spilled dirt around it, patting it with her hands. In no time, the spider plant had a happy new home on Tracy's desk.

Julie followed Tracy back down the hall to the kitchen with her tape recorder. "Now can I tape you?" she asked.

"No. I have an important call to make." Tracy took the phone off the kitchen wall and stretched the cord down the hall into her room, shutting the door.

"Mom says we're not allowed to stretch the phone cord!" Julie said to the closed door.

The twisted phone cord peeked out from under Tracy's door and snaked down the hallway. It reminded

Julie of a stretched-out Slinky, and it gave her an idea. If Tracy wouldn't take the time to be interviewed, the tape would just have to come to Tracy!

Feeling like Harriet the Spy, Julie tiptoed down the hall to her mother's bedroom. Tape recorder in hand, she gingerly picked up the other extension and soundlessly placed the microphone next to the receiver. Then she tiptoed back to her room. Julie could picture Tracy sitting at her window seat, twirling a strand of hair around her finger as she chit-chatted with her friend.

After what felt like forever, Julie heard her sister hang the phone back up in the kitchen. She sneaked past Tracy's closed door, hung up the extension in Mom's room, grabbed the tape recorder, and made a dash for the safety of her own room.

Her closet was the only place that afforded Julie the extra privacy she needed to listen to her secret tape. She switched on the closet light, hit rewind, and adjusted the volume to low.

At first, Tracy's talk with her friend Suzanne was just boring stuff about kids Julie didn't know, such as which girls liked which boys and what to wear to some dance. Then, halfway into the conversation, Julie couldn't believe her ears. She hit rewind and played it again.

A secret like this was too big to hold in. A secret like this—especially when it was about your big sister—was meant to be shared.

Julie peeked out of her bedroom door. The coast was clear. She ran to the kitchen and dialed Ivy's number, stretching the cord all the way to her room this time, ignoring the warning she'd given Tracy a little while ago.

"Hey, Ivy. It's me. Want to hear a super-duper juicy secret?"

"Sure! That's what friends are for, isn't it?"

Both girls giggled nervously. "It's not about me," Julie explained. "It's about Tracy. I got it on tape. Listen to this. But you have to promise you won't tell. Cross your heart?"

"Of course I won't tell! What is it?"

Julie pushed the play button and held the phone receiver up to the tape recorder.

Suzanne: When did this happen?

Tracy: At the movies last Saturday. I went to see

Jaws with a bunch of kids from the tennis team, but I like this one boy, Matt, so I made Jill switch seats so I could sit next to him.

Suzanne: What did Matt do?

Tracy: Well, first I thought he didn't even like me. But he did share his SweeTarts with me. Then, the next thing I knew, there's this long part where they're on the boat, and it's real quiet, and . . .

Suzanne: Yeah, yeah, what happened?

Tracy: He reached over and held my hand, just like that. I was so surprised I almost swallowed my gum.

Suzanne: (squealing) He held your hand?

Tracy: Yeah! I thought everything was going great, but then, right after the movie, he told me I chewed my gum too loud during the scary parts.

Suzanne: He said that? Rude!

Julie hit stop. "Ivy, could you hear all that? My sister has a boyfriend! Tracy and Matt, sitting in a tree," Julie chanted.

"Yuck, I can't believe she really likes a boy."

"Yep, and I know who he is, too. I've seen him at Tracy's tennis matches. He has really blond hair and peach fuzz on his lip that looks like a milk mustache."

"Gross!" said Ivy. "Are you going to tell her you know?"

"Well, if I do, she'll ask how I found out. She'd never believe it was just by chance. Still, it would be a waste not to bug her about it *some*how!"

Julie was singing a song into her microphone and dancing around her room after dinner when Tracy poked her head in the doorway.

"Knock-knock," said Tracy. "I hate to interrupt the concert, but Mom says she could really use our help downstairs in the shop. She got a whole shipment of night-lights today."

"I'll help," said Julie, dropping her microphone on the bed. She pushed past Tracy and headed down the back steps. "Last one there's a rotten egg," she shouted as she raced down the stairs ahead of Tracy.

Mom set two big boxes on the back worktable. "Girls, can you unpack these night-lights? Be careful with the seashells. We have to put them together first, then price each one."

Julie lifted some delicate shells out of the box.

"Wow, look at this shell," she said, holding up a round purplish globe. "It almost looks like a starfish on top."

"That's a sea urchin," said Mom. "It works like a mini lampshade." Mom showed them how to assemble one of the night-lights, carefully placing the globe over a small night-light bulb and then plugging it in to make sure it worked.

When Mom flicked off the overhead lamp, the soft light cast delicate patterns on the shadowy wall. The magical light transported Julie back to Christmas when she was little. In her mind's eye, she saw herself, Mom, and Tracy stringing popcorn by the twinkling lights of the Christmas tree, while Dad stood on a stepladder pinning the star to the very top of the tree.

"I want one of these for my room," said Tracy, breaking the spell.

"I can make you a really good deal," said Mom, chuckling.

The girls set to work assembling the night-lights and putting a price sticker on the bottom of each one. Julie loved handling the pretty seashells and trying to decide which shape she liked best. She felt like an elf in Santa's workshop. What fun it was, to be helping Mom in the back of the shop after hours! It occurred to her that if her parents hadn't split up, her mother might never have opened Gladrags. Julie sighed, confused. How could she feel so torn between the way things used to be and the way her life was now?

Tracy pulled a conch shell out of the box. All of a sudden, she put one hand up to her forehead, making a fin, and sang, "*Dun-dun*! *Dun-dun, dun-dun*!" in a deep, ominous, hollow-drum-sounding voice.

Julie tilted her head, looking puzzled.

"It's the music from the movie *Jaws*," Tracy explained. "You know, the great white shark. Don't go in the water," she warned in a creepy voice, then reached out to grab Julie's leg.

"Aaah!" screamed Julie, almost dropping one of the fragile shells.

"Girls, be careful. These break easily," Mom cautioned.

"So, you liked the movie?" Julie casually asked.

"Yeah. I'm going to go see it again," said Tracy.

"I didn't think *Jaws* was still playing in theaters," Mom said.

"There's this one theater in San Francisco that

still plays it all the time," said Tracy. "And everybody screams when the shark attacks, no matter how many times they've seen it." Tracy turned back to the night-lights. "They made a giant model of a shark for the movie," she added. "It's called Bruce."

"How do you know that?" asked Julie.

"My friend told me. He got the poster with a picture of it at the theater," said Tracy.

"He?" asked Julie. "As in *boy*friend?"

"Grow up," said Tracy. "When you're in high school, you can have friends that are boys. It's no big deal."

Tracy was always acting so superior! Well, for once Tracy wasn't the only one with special, *insider* knowledge.

"Did you get anything to eat at the movies?" Julie asked.

"Not really," said Tracy.

"Not even gum?" Julie pressed.

"Huh? What are you talking about?"

"Oh, I was just thinking about how it's fun to chew gum at the movies—like during the scary parts, it helps to not be scared if you chew your gum *real loud*."

Tracy opened her eyes wide and shot Julie a look. A how-do-you-know-that, you'd-better-not-say-another-word look. Julie could see the machinery of Tracy's mind turning it over like a tricky math problem as she struggled to figure out how Julie knew about the gum.

"My, you girls sure are quiet all of a sudden," Mom remarked.

"Mom, how much longer do you think this will take? I have homework," said Tracy. "Julie does, too, don't you?" Tracy challenged her younger sister with her eyes.

"Go on up," said Mom. "You girls were really a big help tonight. Thank you."

The second they got to the top of the stairs, Tracy turned on Julie, wagging an accusing finger at her. "You eavesdropped on me! You listened right outside my door when I was on the phone with Suzanne, didn't you? Admit it."

"I did not. I was nowhere near your room when you were on the phone. I was right here almost the whole time," said Julie, walking into her room and pointing to her bed.

Tracy followed her. "What was all that about the gum, then?"

"I have homework, remember?" said Julie, plopping down on her bed.

"I'm not leaving till you tell me what you heard."

"How's Matt the gnat?" Julie teased.

"Oh!" Tracy huffed, hands on her hips. "You, you—" she stuttered, but words wouldn't come out.

"Tra-cy has a boy-friend," Julie teased in a sing-song voice.

"I do not! You better not tell anybody!"

"Do too! I have proof, right here." Julie popped out the cassette tape and held it up, taunting her sister.

"Who do you think you are, Little Miss Watergate? Give me that tape," said Tracy, reaching over and snatching it out of Julie's hand.

"Hey, that's my homework. Give it back!"

Tracy held the tape out of Julie's reach. "Don't you know it's illegal to tape someone without telling them?"

It was? Julie felt a twinge of guilt, but she mustered a comeback anyway. "So, what are you going to do, call the police?"

Tracy hesitated, glaring at her sister, then tossed the tape on the floor. Julie snatched it up.

"You better not tell anyone about this!" Tracy hissed through clenched teeth. "I mean it, Julie." She stomped out of the room, and Julie heard the angry slam of

Tracy's door down the hall.

Just then, Mom came into Julie's room with a startled look. "What was that all about?"

"Nothing," said Julie. "Mom, what's Watergate?"

"A few years ago, President Nixon hired people to spy on his political opponents. When he got caught, he lied and tried to cover it up. But some secret tapes revealed that he was lying, so he resigned from being president. That's why Gerald Ford is our president now." Mom raised her eyebrows. "Why do you ask?"

"Tracy just called me Little Miss Watergate. But I wasn't lying about anything," Julie said innocently. "I was just trying to tape her for my project."

Mom gave Julie a serious look. "It's okay for your school project," she said, "*if* you have her permission. But otherwise, I don't want you bothering your sister with that tape recorder."

This Little Piggy

CHAPTER 9

At school the next day, Ms. Hunter took the class to the library to read biographies. Julie chose a biography of Clara Barton and sat down next to T. J.

"What'd you get?" she whispered. He held up a book about Daniel Boone.

Julie looked down at her book and tried to concentrate on the words she was reading: "Clara Barton, angel of the Civil War battlefield, watched over her patients as the surgeon dressed their wounds with cornhusks."

She tried not to look at T. J. One look at her friend and she knew she'd start giggling. But finally she turned to T. J. again.

"Are you going to be at practice today after school?" she whispered.

"Of course. It's only two weeks to the big game."

"Yikes! Two weeks till we play the Wildcats," Julie whispered.

"They're undefeated," said T. J. "And they have this one player—"

"Class," said Ms. Hunter, "remember what I said about visiting with your neighbor. This is supposed to be silent reading."

After basketball practice, Coach Manley called the team into a huddle. "Johnson, work on that defense inside the key. Albright, I've seen notes in class passed faster than your bounce pass. McDermott, what's with all the fouls? Tomorrow you'd better be over your case of the clumsies. That's it, players. See you tomorrow."

As soon as Coach Manley was out of earshot, T. J. muttered, "What got into Coach today? I feel like I just ran a marathon or something."

"What's wrong with my defense, anyway?" complained Paul Johnson, point guard for the Jaguars.

"And I had one of my best passes ever," Julie chimed in. "I think Coach Manley needs glasses."

"He's just uptight about playing the Wildcats.

He thinks we're not ready to take them on," said Tommy McDermott, the team captain.

"At this rate, we're going to be too *tired* to play the Wildcats," said T. J., and everybody laughed.

"I hear they have this one fifth grader who's practically six feet tall," said Tony Monteverdi, who played center. "They call him Dunk because he can jam balls right through the hoop."

"Yeah, he thinks he's the next Kareem Abdul-Jabbar," said Brian Hannigan, the team's forward. Brian was five foot eight himself, but even he looked worried.

"Great," said Julie. "I bet he's just going to love playing against a team with a girl."

"Hey, don't go thinking that way," said Paul. "You're one of the best ball handlers we've got on this team. We don't call you Cool Hand Albright for nothing."

"Really? You guys gave me a nickname?"

"Are you kidding?" said T. J. "You can dribble rings around half this team."

All the way home, Julie couldn't stop thinking about the Wildcats. Just the thought of going up against the legendary Dunk made her shiver. To chase away the goose bumps, Julie recalled Paul's words. *One of the best ball handlers.* She could still feel the warm glow of the compliment.

Cool Hand Albright. Her very own nickname!

On Saturday morning, Julie set up an obstacle course on the sidewalk with a laundry basket, an empty scrub bucket, and a family-sized box of detergent. She weaved her way in and out of the obstacles, switching hands, practicing her dribbling, then pretending to palm off the ball in a bounce pass to an imaginary player.

"Hey! Whatya doing?" a voice asked. Tracy.

"Practicing my bounce pass. Coach Manley told me it needs work."

"Well, it looks pretty good to me," said Tracy cheerfully. "Want me to stand in? You can go through the course, then pass the ball off to me."

"Hey, wait a minute," said Julie. "I thought you weren't talking to me. Now you're trying to help me with basketball? What's up?"

"Nothing," said Tracy. "I'm over it. Besides, I can't stay mad at my little sister forever, can I?" She leaned in and gave Julie a sideways hug.

"I'm not doing the dishes for you tonight, if that's what you're thinking," Julie replied.

"No, of course not," said Tracy. "C'mon, why don't you start dribbling, then pass the ball to me."

"Well, okay, thanks. Ready?" asked Julie.

For the next several minutes, Julie weaved, turned, faked, and drove the ball this way and that, bounce-passing it to Tracy, who passed it right back. In the scramble, Tracy kicked over the bucket and Julie knocked into the detergent, spilling white powder all over the sidewalk. Between bounce passes, Tracy tried to steal the ball, but Julie was too fast.

"Time out!" Tracy called, winded. The two girls gulped in air and sat down on a nearby front step.

"By the way," Tracy said, absentmindedly curling a strand of hair around her finger, "you know how you've been dying to babysit?"

"Yeah, but Mom says I'm still too young," Julie replied. "Why? You know somebody who needs a babysitter?"

"Umm—sort of."

"Who?" Julie bolted upright, excited by the possibility of her first job. "When can I start? Do you think

Mom'll let me? How much do they pay?"

"Well, since it's your first time, it would have to be for free. You know, to get experience. Then you work up to the big bucks."

"I don't know," said Julie, leaning back on her elbows. "On *The Brady Bunch,* Marcia and Greg get their parents to pay them just to babysit their own brothers and sisters."

"Well, this isn't *The Brady Bunch,*" said Tracy. "Could you start later today?"

"You mean it? For real? How old is the kid? What's the kid's name?"

Tracy hesitated. She glanced sideways at Julie. "Charlotte?" she said, making it sound like a question.

"It's your plant!" Julie said in disbelief. "You want me to babysit a dumb old plant? That's why you're being all nice and helping me with basketball and everything?"

"C'mon, Jules, you'd really be helping me out. It's super easy—you'd hardly have to do anything. Just go in my room and check on it a couple times while I'm gone. If the soil feels dry, give it a little water. And if you notice anything different or unusual, just write it down so that I can record it in my science journal."

"I can't. Ivy's coming for a sleepover, and I might forget. Besides, what's so important that you can't do it yourself? You're probably just hanging out with your friends at the Doggy Diner."

"Not this time," said Tracy. She lowered her voice to a conspiratorial whisper. "See, I'm going to my friend Jill's house with a bunch of people, and her brother has a VW bug. Have you ever heard of Volkswagen stuffing? We're going to see how many kids we can pile into one little VW bug. It's like playing Twister times ten."

"That sounds weird," said Julie.

"It's going to be crazy fun," said Tracy, "and Jill invited me to spend the night at her house. I really want to go, but I'll get points marked off if I skip two whole days in my journal."

"I never heard of such a dopey idea—babysitting a plant."

"Sure, it's called plant-sitting. You can make a lot of money taking care of people's houseplants when they go away."

"Really? Plant-sitting, huh? Okay, I'll do it. But it'll cost you. Two dollars."

"Two dollars! Are you nuts? For maybe watering it

once and making sure it doesn't croak?"

"Take it or leave it," said Julie, crossing her arms to show that her mind was made up.

"One dollar," said Tracy.

"Deal," said Julie.

"The eensy-weensy spider went up the water spout," Julie sang to the plant on her bedroom windowsill. Ivy joined in, adding all the hand motions that went with the song.

"Tell me again why we're singing to a plant?" Ivy asked.

"It's for Tracy's science project. She asked me to watch her plant this weekend, but I was afraid I'd forget, so I just brought it in here. There's more sunlight in my room, anyway," said Julie. "And I read in a magazine that if you sing to plants or play music around them, they grow faster."

"Really? That sounds wacky," said Ivy.

"I know," Julie admitted. "But wouldn't it be great if Tracy came back and her plant had grown a whole inch? She'd get extra credit for sure. Let's sing it again!"

"Okay, one last time," Ivy agreed. "Then let's go do something outside."

"I know—this time I'll tape us singing!" said Julie. "Then I can just play the tape for Charlotte."

When the girls were finished singing, Julie pressed the play button and then picked up her basketball. "Want to go shoot some hoops?"

"Sure," said Ivy. "Let me get my shoes on."

"Think fast!" Julie said, tossing a pass to Ivy. But Ivy had bent down to pull on her boots. The ball hit the dresser, rattling Julie's gumball machine, then zinged off the corner, heading right for the open window.

"Noooooo!" Julie dove across the bed, lunging to save the ball from going out the window. The basketball thumped against the windowsill, then bounced into Julie's hands. "Whew—got it!"

Ivy stared at the window in horror.

Crash.

"What was that?" Julie followed Ivy's gaze to the open window—and empty windowsill.

For a split second, Julie's mouth gaped open in shock. Then Julie and Ivy rushed over to the window and peered down at the sidewalk below. Charlotte lay in a jumbled heap on the ground. Dirt was scattered all over the sidewalk. The clay hippo was smashed to pieces.

In a blur, Julie and Ivy raced down the back steps and out onto the sidewalk.

"Oh, no!" said Julie, covering her face in disbelief. "What are we going to do?" She picked up the spider plant, turning it in her hand. Many of the long, blade-like leaves were crushed and broken, and the roots looked pale and limp.

"Maybe the roots are still okay," Ivy said hopefully. "And we can clean up all this dirt. It's probably still perfectly good dirt."

"But the pot—we've got to put it back together."

Ivy shook her head. "There are too many pieces. We'll never be able to glue it."

"Then we'll have to find another pot just like it," said Julie, picking up the pieces.

"Does your mom have more pots like this at her shop?" Ivy asked.

"No, that's the problem. This one was just a sample," Julie explained.

"I've seen them at the Five-and-Ten Shop in

Chinatown," said Ivy. "My mom has one that's a frog."

"Hey, there's a Five-and-Ten Shop right down on Haight Street," said Julie, brushing the last of the dirt off the sidewalk. "Let me use your bag to carry Charlotte in. I'll tell my mom we're going. Come on!"

On Haight Street, the girls rushed past the bead shop, the record store, and the art-supply store. At the antique store, Ivy paused to admire a silk kimono on a mannequin in the window, while Julie peeked at Charlotte, who lay in a soft bag that was made from an old pair of blue jeans. Charlotte looked a bit crushed.

"Mom's told me a million times not to throw the basketball in the house. Now I know why," Julie murmured. "Come on, we better hurry."

At the Five-and-Ten Shop, Ivy followed Julie past a pyramid of Charlie perfume and down an aisle filled with old Halloween candy.

"There's the plant section," Julie said, motioning to Ivy. They walked past rows of African violets and begonias, looking for the pots.

"Over there!" said Ivy. "I see one that's a turtle." They scanned the cluttered shelf, searching for a planter in the shape of a hippo, like Tracy's.

"They have bunnies and puppies, cows and kittens," said Julie. "There just has to be a hippo." She began lifting out all the pots stacked behind the front row and setting them on the floor.

"May I help you?" asked a tall woman wearing a blue smock with a name tag that said "Glenda." She peered at them over glasses attached to a chain around her neck.

"Sorry," said Julie. "We'll put these all back. We're just looking for a hippo."

"It's an emergency," Ivy explained.

"The puppies are very cute," said Glenda. "They're our most popular item."

Both girls shook their heads. "It has to be a hippo."

"I don't think we've ever carried a hippo, but we might be able to order one," Glenda offered.

"You don't understand," said Julie. "This is my sister's plant, for a school project. She had it in a hippo planter, and I broke it!"

"Oh, I think I'm getting the picture. Tell you what. We have a few piggies left, over here," Glenda said, lifting one down from a high-up shelf. "Don't you think it looks a bit like a hippo?"

Julie looked at Ivy. Ivy shrugged. "It's pretty close," she told her friend.

"We could even call it Wilbur, like the pig in *Charlotte's Web.* But not to Tracy, of course," said Julie. She turned to Glenda. "Okay, we'll take it."

"Would you like me to pot it up for you?" Glenda asked, glancing at the limp plant in Julie's hand. "I can trim off some of those broken leaves."

"Really? That'd be great. Does it cost extra?"

"Not for emergencies." Glenda winked at Julie. "I'll have to take it in the back. Why don't you girls look around and come back in fifteen minutes?"

While they waited, Julie and Ivy wandered over to the pet section. They tried to get the parakeets to talk, watched two hamsters run a race on their wheels, and gazed at the hermit crabs, hoping to catch one changing shells. At the turtle tank, they made up names for some of the baby turtles, like Slow Poke and Cutie Pie. One turtle had gotten stuck on its back, so the girls reached in and helped it to flip over.

"Julie and Ivy to the rescue!" said Ivy.

"It's probably been fifteen minutes," said Julie. "Let's go see if Wilbur and Charlotte are ready."

At the counter, Glenda handed them the spider plant. "Well, I can't say it's good as new, but it should pull through. Be sure to give it a good drink when you get home."

"Thanks a million!" said Julie as she paid for the pot. "It looks better already."

"And the leaves cover up the pot, so you can't really tell it's not a hippo," said Ivy.

"Be careful now," said Glenda, waving. "You don't want to make any more trips to the plant hospital today."

The girls smiled and waved good-bye as they headed out the door. "Time for this little piggy to go home!" said Julie.

❀

The next afternoon, Julie and Ivy sat with their legs folded under them at the kitchen table, riveted to the tick-tick-ticking of the cat's tail on the Kit-Kat Klock hanging above the stove.

"Quit looking at the clock. You're making me nervous," said Julie, turning back to their game of Chinese checkers.

"The way the cat's eyeballs move back and forth,

I feel like he's staring at me," said Ivy, jumping a marble twice. "Do you think Tracy's going to know something happened to her plant?"

"I hope not. Because if that plant dies, she might flunk her assignment."

"Uh-oh," said Ivy.

"Speaking of assignments, one *good* thing about all this is I have a new idea for my report. Best Thing Ever: my first paid plant-sitting job. Worst Thing Ever: knocking Charlotte out the window." Julie moved a marble into her home triangle. "Remember, when Tracy gets here, just act natural."

"Don't worry," said Ivy. "She'll be so busy thinking about dreamboat Matt, she probably won't even notice."

Five minutes later, the front door opened, and Tracy called out, "Hey, everybody. I'm ba-ack!"

"Good, sounds like she's in a good mood," Julie whispered to Ivy.

"Anybody home?" Tracy called.

"We're in the kitchen," Julie called back. She swallowed hard and stared at the marbles on the board as her sister entered the room.

"Hi, Ivy," said Tracy.

"So, did you and your friends break any world records?" asked Julie. "You know, for the number of people in a Volkswagen?"

"I think we broke the record for the number of *squished* people," said Tracy. "So, anything happening around here?"

"No!" Julie glanced nervously at Ivy, who was rolling a marble between her fingers. "What makes you say that?"

"Nothing, I was just asking," said Tracy. She picked up her backpack. "Well, I'm going to go change."

"She didn't even ask about Charlotte," Julie whispered when Tracy had left the room.

Suddenly they heard a shriek. Tracy's door flew open and she yelled down the hall, "Julie, what in the world did you do?"

Julie hurried to Tracy's room, with Ivy right behind her. "What do you mean? What's wrong?" she asked.

Tracy pointed at the spider plant on her desk. "My plant looks *smaller.* Like it shrunk. And the tips of the leaves are turning brown! Are you sure you watered it, like I said?" Tracy asked.

"Positive. We held it under the faucet for like five minutes. Didn't we, Ivy?"

Ivy bit her lip and nodded. "Yeah, and we put it in Julie's window so it would get more sunlight. We sang to it, too."

"Great, you probably overwatered it. Plants can drown, you know. And it's not supposed to be in direct sunlight. No wonder the tips are brown!"

"Maybe some music will help," said Julie. "We made Charlotte a tape—want us to play it?"

"Never mind," said Tracy with a heavy sigh. "I'll just have to put these observations in my journal."

Julie and Ivy wandered back to the kitchen table and gazed at the Chinese checkers board.

"I think it's your move," said Julie, but the game no longer seemed fun.

"Hey, she didn't even notice Wilbur," said Ivy.

"Yeah," said Julie. "That's good, at least."

The Big Game

CHAPTER 10

Three more days. Two more days. One more day. Julie deliberately marked a red crayon X through each day leading up to the big game with the Wildcats, the Thursday that had been circled on her calendar for the last three weeks.

All of a sudden, Julie came up with a new idea for her report.

Best Thing Ever: the big game was finally here.

Worst Thing Ever: the big game was really and truly here! *Aaieee!*

She looked in the mirror and took a deep breath, willing herself steady. Uniform? Check. Sneakers? Check. Tube socks? Check. Sweatband? Check. Julie stuffed the items she'd need into her gym bag, double- and triple-checking to make sure she had everything.

"All ready?" asked Mom, poking her head into

Julie's room. "I made French toast this morning. Thought you could use a real breakfast for your big day. And I put some granola bars in your lunch in case you need some quick energy after school before the game."

"Thanks, Mom." Julie's voice came out in a tiny squeak.

"Nervous?" asked Mom.

"A little," said Julie. "Excited, too. I just wish you could be there."

"I know, honey. I'm disappointed, too. Of all the days for the bank to schedule a big meeting to talk about my business loan. But Dad'll be there. I'm sure he'll take some pictures. And you can tell me all about it, play by play."

Mom drove Julie to school that morning and gave her an extra-special squeeze before Julie got out of the car. "Remember, take a deep breath, and just do your best. That's all anybody can ask."

"See ya later, Hoopster," said Tracy, sliding out of the front bench seat so Julie could climb out. "Go easy on those boys, now. Don't make those Wildcats look too bad." Julie giggled. "I'll try to be there by the second half, if tennis practice is over," Tracy told her.

"Bye!" Julie waved.

"One, two, three . . . Go, Jaguars!" Julie, T. J., and the other players broke from the huddle, and the big game was on. The opening jump ball went to the Wildcats, and it was all the Jaguars could do to keep up. Elbows were flying and feet racing, and the crowd was already up out of their seats, cheering as the ball moved up and down the court.

"Defense, defense!" Coach Manley yelled to his players.

Julie double-teamed with T. J. to try to block the tall kid, Wildcat Number 16, also known as Dunk.

"Hey, 22, forget your cheerleading pom-poms?" Dunk snickered as he stole the ball out from under Julie. Then he elbowed right past her, shoving her out of the way. It was the third time he had fouled her, but the ref had only called a foul once.

"Hey, no fair," Julie called.

"That's a foul, 'fraidy-cats!" T. J. shouted.

Julie knew her dad worried about rough playing,

and he would not be happy about it. She tried to spot him in the stands, but the game was moving fast and she couldn't find him.

Julie ran downcourt. With a minute left in the first half, the Jaguars were down by six points, but they had the ball.

"Hey, ballerina," called Number 16. "Where's your tutu?"

Julie gritted her teeth. She had to concentrate, focus, do everything Coach Manley had taught them in practice to block out distractions and drive the ball so that her team could score.

Then Dunk was on her again, so she quickly passed the ball to T. J. He was instantly surrounded and had to pass the ball back. Just as the ball reached Julie's hands, Dunk lunged, grasping for the ball and knocking Julie flat on the floor.

The shrill sound of the ref's whistle stopped the game. Julie curled up on the court, holding her hand close to her chest in pain. Next thing she knew, she was being helped off the court, and Tracy was at her side.

"Where's Dad?" Julie asked in a shaky voice.

"You mean he's not here?" Tracy said. "I just got

here myself. Are you okay?"

"Let's have a look at that hand," said Coach Manley. He was already calling for ice and a first-aid kit.

"It's my finger. It bent back under me when I was pushed down. I can't move it."

"Yeah, you have some swelling, all right. We'll ice it, and we need to get you to the emergency room and have it looked at," said Coach Manley. "Better get an X-ray to be on the safe side."

"Leave the game? Please, no!" If she left the game now, people would *really* think that girls shouldn't play basketball. "Coach, can't we tape it up or something so that I can stay in? Can I at least make my foul shot?"

"No. I hope it's just a sprain, but I'm not taking any chances," said Coach Manley. "Is your mom or dad here?"

"Just my sister," said Julie.

"Our dad's supposed to be here," said Tracy, "but I don't see him anywhere."

T. J. was standing right next to Julie. "My mom's here. She could take you," he offered, running over to the bleachers to alert his mother.

Tracy helped Julie out through the gym door, and the sounds of the clapping, cheering crowd began to fade as they walked down the empty hall and out the front doors of the school. Clutching her injured finger to her chest, Julie couldn't help thinking that leaving the game hurt almost as much as the pulsing and throbbing of her swollen finger.

Julie sat tense and rigid in a straight-backed chair in the hospital waiting room. Holding ice to her purple, swollen finger, she fought back the tears.

"Are you okay, honey?" T. J.'s mother asked, putting her hand on Julie's shoulder. "Can I get you anything?"

"Just my mom and dad," Julie sniffed, trying to put on a good face. So much for Cool Hand Albright. How could her hand have let her down like this?

"Tracy's calling them now, and by the time you get done with the doctor, I'm sure they'll be here," said T. J.'s mother.

"You don't understand," said Julie. "My mom and dad don't live together anymore. They're . . . divorced. My dad was supposed to be at the game, and I don't know what happened. Tracy already called Mom twice and can't reach her, either."

"Well, I'll stay with you girls until we reach one of your parents. Don't you worry about that. Right now, we just need to get you in to the doctor and feeling better."

Just then, Tracy came back from using the pay phone.

"Any luck?" T. J.'s mother asked Tracy.

"Still no answer. Mom had to go to a meeting at the bank today. She must not be back yet, and I don't know which bank it is. My dad has a new answering machine, so I left him a message on it. I guess I'll just keep trying."

"Julie Albright," called a nurse, looking down at her clipboard. "Julie Albright."

Julie and Tracy spent nearly an hour behind a curtain at the emergency room while the doctor took X-rays of Julie's finger. Then he listened to her heart, looked into her ears, and shone a bright beam of light in her eyes. By the time she emerged, her arm was resting safely in a sling, and her broken finger was splinted and taped to its neighbor so that she couldn't bend it or move it.

Julie and Tracy both looked up and down the waiting area, trying to spot T. J.'s mom.

"There she is," a familiar voice exclaimed. Dad! Julie looked up. Rushing down the hall toward her were Mom *and* Dad. Together.

They hurried over to Julie, enfolding her in one big hug. All the tears that she'd been holding back came out in a flood of relief.

"Honey, honey, we just heard. Are you okay?" Mom asked, dabbing tears from Julie's face with the corner of her scarf. "Does it hurt? You girls must have been so scared," she said, looking up at Tracy. "Thank you so much," she added, turning to T. J.'s mother.

"We got here as fast as we could," said Dad, kneeling down to take a closer look at Julie's finger and splint. "What happened? Is anything broken?"

"We were at Julie's basketball game," said Tracy. "This big kid from the other team kept pushing Julie. He wouldn't leave her alone—"

"And they weren't even calling it a foul," added Julie, finding words coming back to her. "Then next thing I knew, he knocked into me, and I fell and landed on my finger. It bent way back the wrong way and hurt really bad and—"

"She broke her finger!" Tracy interrupted, looking back and forth from Mom to Dad.

"Except the doctor kept calling it a *phalange,*" said Julie. "Now I'm like a robot," she added, holding up her splinted finger to show off all the metal and gauze around it.

"We'll take care of your finger, and it'll heal soon," Mom reassured her. "I'm just so sorry this happened."

"We're very proud of both of you girls," said Dad. "Tracy, honey, I know this was a lot for you to handle—"

"Where were you, Dad?" Tracy snapped. "Weren't you supposed to be there? What if I hadn't made it to the game after tennis?" Tracy's voice was shaking.

"Tracy," Mom said gently, "your father had a weather delay out of Chicago, and there was nothing he could do. These things happen, and it's nobody's fault. We're all just relieved that Julie's okay."

"I tried to call you a bunch of times," Tracy accused Mom.

"I know," said Mom. "It's a good thing Dad got that answering machine. He got your message and called me right away, and we came here just as soon as we could. You did the right thing, honey. I know how scary it is when you're worried like that." Mom pulled Tracy closer, stroking her hair.

"You came with Dad? Together? In the same car?" Julie asked.

"Yes, honey, we did. Dad picked me up on the way." Mom smiled, and Tracy seemed to relax a bit.

A nurse came over and checked Julie's splint one final time, marking something on her clipboard. "Looks like you're good to go," she announced.

"Anybody hungry?" asked Dad, taking a deep breath and rubbing his hands together. "What do you say we head out and stop for pizza?"

"You mean it?" Julie asked. "Can I, Mom?"

"I mean all of us," Dad said. "It's been a rough day for everybody, and I think we could all use a break. What do you say?"

"I don't mind not cooking tonight," said Mom.

"And I can't do the dishes anyway!" said Julie, pointing to her sling.

Julie looked over at Tracy, afraid she would refuse Dad's invitation. *Say yes, say yes,* Julie pleaded silently.

"I guess," said Tracy. "But only if we go to our old

place in North Beach, so I can order the Very, Very Veggie pizza."

"Now, Tracy—" Mom started.

"It's okay," said Dad. "I don't mind driving us over there, then dropping you all back at your place. We can get two pizzas, so you can each choose your favorite. How about that?"

"Wow," said Julie, looking from Mom to Dad. "I should break my finger more often!"

The Best Thing Ever

❀ CHAPTER 11 ❀

It felt funny to be home resting on the couch on a school day, playing Kerplunk with Mom all morning. Mom had told Julie she could stay home for a day, since it was Friday, and the doctor had recommended taking it easy for a few days. With her uninjured left hand, Julie gingerly extracted a red stick from the marble-filled tower without upsetting a single marble. "Your turn, Mom," she said. "Bet you go *ker-plunk!*"

Mom smiled. "Honey, do you think we could finish the game later? I need to open the shop for at least a few hours today."

"You're not just saying that because you're about to get clobbered, are you, Mom?" Julie teased.

"Boy, nothing gets past you," said Mom. "Now, will you be all right by yourself for a little while? I'm right downstairs if you need me. Come on down if you feel up to it."

"I should probably stay and work on my report. It's due on Monday. I have most of it on tape, but I haven't started writing it down yet. Hey, wait a minute—how am I going to write?" Julie asked, holding up her splinted finger. With all the adhesive tape wrapped around it, Julie thought it looked mummified.

"Hmm, that is going to be a problem," said Mom. "Do you want me to write a note to Ms. Hunter and ask if you can turn it in late?"

"I have a better idea," beamed Julie, jumping up off the sofa. "What if I could turn in my report on tape? I have a lot of it done that way, and I could finish it up without having to write anything."

"Sounds like a creative solution to me," said Mom. "And that way you won't fall behind. I'll call Ms. Hunter and talk to her about it Monday morning."

"Thanks, Mom," Julie said.

Julie spent the rest of the morning editing her project, erasing certain parts of the tape (Tracy's telephone call about Matt) and adding in a few peppy introductions. "Coming up next: the exciting adventures of my dad, daredevil pilot Daniel Albright, when he was my same age. Hold on to your seats!"

Scanning down the list of topics for her project, Julie's finger stopped at the Best Thing That Ever Happened. She had planned to tell about the petition and getting onto the boys' basketball team. Momentarily, she was warmed by the memory of last night—being together as a family again, all four of them, the way it used to be. As if nothing had ever changed. Being a family again last night was possibly the Best Thing That Ever Happened. But if she were to include *that* in her report, it meant she would have to mention the Worst Thing.

When it came to the Worst Thing That Ever Happened, it seemed even harder to say the word *divorce* out loud onto a tape than to write it down. Julie turned on the tape recorder and pushed the record button. She held the microphone up to her face, but no words came.

"The worst thing that ever happened to me," Julie finally stammered, "was when . . ." She couldn't finish her sentence. Giving up, she pressed the stop button. *Great,* thought Julie. *Now I have to turn in a tape with nothing but air at the end.*

Feeling discouraged, Julie stared at her broken finger. Hey, wait a minute—breaking a finger was a bad thing that had happened to her. Not finishing the biggest basketball game of the season was a bad thing that had happened. Julie didn't even have to say a word about the divorce. Her broken finger could be the Worst Thing That Ever Happened.

Julie turned the tape player back on, pushed the record button, and held up the microphone. In a strong voice like a radio announcer, she told the whole story of the Best Thing Ever—the time she collected one hundred fifty signatures on a petition that convinced the principal and school board to let her play on the boys' basketball team. Then, for the Worst Thing Ever, she recounted the game against the Wildcats, complete with her trip to the hospital and her freakish Frankenstein of a finger.

Just as Julie was finishing up her tape, Tracy came home from school. She plopped down on the sofa with her tennis racket.

"How was school today?" Julie started.

"You sound like Mom," said Tracy.

"No, I mean, didn't you have to turn in your science journal today?" Julie asked nervously.

"Yep. And guess what? I got an A. Even though my plant died."

Julie let out a small breath and sank back into the sofa with relief. "Tracy?" she said tentatively. "There's something I have to tell you."

Tracy set down her tennis racket. "What is it?"

"You know that time I watched your plant for you?" said Julie. "Well, I—um, I knocked it out the window by mistake. It was an accident, honest! I was afraid you'd be mad at me and flunk your assignment, so I got a new planter and tried to fix it."

"I know," said Tracy.

"You mean you knew all this time?"

Tracy cocked her head. "I figured you broke the pot. Did you really think I wouldn't be able to tell the difference between a hippo and a pig?"

"I guess not," said Julie in a small voice.

"Why didn't you just tell me what happened instead of going to all that trouble to cover it up?"

Julie squirmed and looked down. "I'm sorry," she said finally. "Really, I am. I was going to tell you before you had to turn in your report, but when you were so mad at Dad yesterday for not being at the game and letting you down, I lost my nerve."

For a few moments, Tracy was quiet, and Julie was afraid her sister was angry. But when Tracy spoke, she just sounded sad. "I know I shouldn't have blown up at Dad. It wasn't his fault he wasn't at the game. But sometimes it's hard not to feel as if—well, as if he's let us down in a really big way. By leaving the family, I mean. By getting divorced." Tracy's voice quivered suddenly, and she turned away.

"But they *both* got divorced," Julie pointed out. "It wasn't just Dad; it was Mom, too. It's not fair to blame the whole thing on Dad."

Tracy was silent. When she turned back to Julie, her eyes were bright, and she blinked a few times to clear them. "You know it's important to tell the truth, Jules." She reached over and tweaked her sister's ponytail. "Besides, we're sisters, and sisters have to stick together. Promise me, next time you'll come talk to me and tell me?"

"Promise," said Julie. She hesitated a moment, then leaned forward and gave Tracy a hug.

On Monday morning, Julie was fumbling and trying to open her locker left-handed when T. J. saw her and called, "Hey, it's Cool Hand Albright. You're back! Let's see the big cast. My mom says you've got mettle, whatever that means."

Julie held up her splint for T. J. to see. "Oh, I've got *metal* all right! Broke my finger. It's not really a cast, just a splint. I'm like the Bionic Woman now."

"Oh, man," said T. J. "I can't believe Dunk ran you over."

"And I can't believe I had to miss the biggest game all season," said Julie. "Thanks for calling to tell me how the rest of the game went. I'm so bummed out we didn't win."

"But we came super close. Coach said we played our best game ever. We probably would have won if they hadn't injured our star player," T. J. teased.

"Thanks," said Julie with a smile. Taking a deep breath, she grabbed her tape recorder with her left hand, slammed her locker shut, and headed for Ms. Hunter's class, hurrying down the hall side by side with T. J.

Everybody buzzed around Julie, talking about the big game and Julie's broken finger. Like the Telephone game, the story had grown with each telling. One student had heard that Julie was rushed to the hospital in an ambulance. Another had heard that her finger got gangrene and had to be cut off! Julie had not been this popular since the day her mother had visited her class for Career Day and had given everybody free bracelets and mood rings.

Ms. Hunter clapped her hands, and the students returned to their seats to listen to one another's reports.

Angela went first. For the Worst Thing That Ever Happened, she told about the time she jumped into the pool and her bathing suit bottom came off. The whole class burst out laughing, and Ms. Hunter had to blink the lights just to get everybody to settle down.

T. J. went next. He called his report "Cheaper by the Half Dozen" and told all about living with five sisters. (Julie couldn't imagine having five sisters—one was plenty.) T. J. described how his mom gave all the kids haircuts to save money. For the girls, she just trimmed a few inches off the ends, but for T. J., she put a bowl on top of his head and cut off all the hair below it. T. J.

showed a picture of himself in second grade, looking like Moe from the Three Stooges.

"Now who's brave," Julie whispered when T. J. sat down. "That took super-duper courage to show everybody that picture!"

Finally, it was Julie's turn. Carrying her tape recorder, she walked to the front of the class. "As everybody knows, I broke my finger on my right hand, so I couldn't write out my report in handwriting," she started to explain.

"Aw, let's have a pity party," one of the students remarked.

"Hey, my finger hurts too," somebody else called out.

Julie laughed. "For real, I had to record my report on tape. So I'm going to play it for you now."

The class listened intently to the stories of Dad's big bike ride, Mom's runaway horse, Charlotte the Spider Plant, and the Best Thing Ever—the petition and playing basketball for the Jaguars. Finally, Julie's voice on the tape said, "And last but not least, I'm going to tell you about the Worst Thing That Ever Happened."

Click. Julie turned off the tape recorder.

"Hey, no fair!" said a boy in the back row. "You have

to let us hear the worst thing. That's the best part!"

Julie looked hesitantly at her teacher. She could feel her palms beginning to sweat, yet her throat felt dry as chalk dust. "Ms. Hunter," she said, trying to swallow, "would it be okay if I just tell the last part aloud, I mean, without the tape? I sort of changed my mind about what I want to say."

"I don't see that as a problem," said Ms. Hunter.

Julie straightened up her slumped shoulders and began. "I was going to play back the story of my broken finger for the Worst Thing That Ever Happened to me," she explained. "But really, that wouldn't be telling the truth. Because even worse than a broken finger is when my family broke apart. A few months ago, my mom and dad decided to get a divorce. That means I don't get to live with both of my parents anymore."

Julie's stomach turned somersaults. She wanted to leave to go get a drink of water, but she forced her feet to stand steady.

"When I broke my finger," she continued, "my mom and dad both came to the hospital. And after I got bandaged up, we all went out for pizza together. I was so happy to have us all back together again that it was almost worth breaking my finger. Except that it only lasted for one night. We weren't together again for real, permanently." Julie paused, thinking what to say next. This time the class was dead quiet, waiting for her to continue.

Julie knew she had covered all the topics for her report, but she realized there was still something she was trying to say. "Just now, as I was playing back the tape, I remembered something my dad told me when he broke his foot. He said that a broken bone heals back together even stronger than before it was broken."

Julie's stomach was feeling less queasy, and her voice was stronger now, more confident. "I think families are kind of like bones—they can break too, but in some ways, it makes you even stronger. And when one person's in trouble or gets hurt, families pull together, and you can still count on them to be there for you.

"The end. That's the Story of My Life. So far."

Everybody clapped. Julie walked down the aisle, back to her seat at the initial-carved desk she'd come to think of as her own. Her heart still pounding, she slid into her chair, aware now of the pulsing in her injured finger. She knew in her heart that the break in her family would always be there. But the love she felt for her sister and her parents, and the love they felt for her, was as strong as ever. That part couldn't be broken.

Changes for Christmas

❀ CHAPTER 12 ❀

ulie's finger healed quickly, and before long she was back on the basketball court. The rest of basketball season flew by. For the elementary teams, it ended in December, when school let out for the holidays. It would be nine whole months, Julie realized, before basketball started up again.

But something else had begun to occupy her thoughts. Christmas had always been her favorite holiday—but now that Mom and Dad were celebrating separately, this year would be different.

"Julie! Tracy! Over here!" A man's voice called her back to the present—the Christmas-tree lot on the corner of San Francisco's Ashbury and Waller Streets. "Hey! Are you my first customers?" It was Hank.

"I wish," said Tracy. "We were on our way to the

bakery when Julie gave all her money to the Salvation Army."

"Just what was in my change purse," said Julie. "I didn't have enough for a Christmas tree anyway."

"Mom and Dad used to take us up to Santa Rosa every year to a Christmas-tree farm near our grandma and grandpa's," Tracy explained.

"And you cut down your own tree!" Julie gushed. "And there's a train you can ride, and you get free apple crisp, and—"

"But not this year," said Tracy, kicking at a stone with her boot. "Mom says money's tight and she has to work around the clock."

"And since we're spending Christmas at Dad's, she says we don't need a tree this year," Julie added glumly.

"How would you girls like to *adopt* a tree for Christmas?" Hank disappeared behind a row of trees. He came out pulling a red wagon that held a perfectly plump tree in a redwood planter, with feathery branches like arms reaching to the sky.

"I bought a live tree to plant outside the Veterans' Center. We could really use some *sprucing* up over there," Hank said with a wink. "You're welcome to take the tree home until I have time to plant it. It'll last indoors for a week or two."

"Really? You mean it?" Julie asked.

"Scout's honor," said Hank, holding up three fingers. "It's ready to go. All you have to do is water it."

"It's perfect," said Tracy.

"Thanks, Hank," said Julie.

The two sisters stepped back to admire the tree that now filled the second-story bay window at the front of the apartment.

"C'mon," said Tracy. "Let's get out the decorations. We can have this tree sparkling before Mom gets done at the shop." It was Mom's first Christmas season at Gladrags, and the holiday shoppers were keeping her busy.

"I don't know where Mom put all the Christmas stuff after the move," said Julie. "Do you?"

Tracy shook her head. "I'll go down and ask her."

"No, wait! Then she'll know—"

"Know what?" asked Mom, coming up the stairs.

"Aw," said Julie. "We got a tree from Hank, and we

were going to surprise you and decorate it so that you wouldn't have to go to any trouble."

"But we couldn't find the ornaments," Tracy added.

"Tell you what," said Mom. "Let's all decorate the tree tonight, after I close up. It'll be fun. But right now, I'm really swamped with customers. Can you two give me a hand?"

"Sure, I can run the cash register," said Tracy.

"And I could gift-wrap," said Julie.

"Fantastic," said Mom. "With your help, I won't have to turn into a grinch after all."

❀

"What a day!" said Mom as Tracy finally flipped the sign on the front door to CLOSED. "I still have to count the money. Why don't you girls go on upstairs and think about what to have for supper."

"Grilled cheese!" said Julie.

"And tomato soup," said Tracy. "We'll make it, Mom."

"Then we decorate," said Julie.

As soon as the supper dishes were cleared, Julie asked again about the ornaments. Mom frowned and thought for a moment, then looked up sheepishly.

"I just remembered—when we moved, I knew we had a lot less storage space here, so I left the Christmas stuff at Dad's."

"What are we gonna do?" asked Julie. "We have this beautiful tree and no ornaments." She lightly touched the tip of one of the branches. "Hey, wait, I know. We could make our own ornaments."

"But we don't even have lights or tinsel or anything," said Tracy.

"We can string popcorn," Mom suggested.

"I guess," Tracy said skeptically. "But what about Grandma's old-fashioned teapot ornament? And the hummingbird with the fancy wings? It doesn't seem like Christmas without those."

"Yeah, and don't forget the green glass pickle you hide every year, Mom," said Julie.

"I like your idea of making ornaments," Mom said.

"Well, I could fold some origami paper cranes," said Julie. "We learned how in school."

Mom smiled and nodded. "Tracy, what about those god's eyes you made out of yarn and chopsticks? They'd brighten up any tree."

"Mom, I made those in Girl Scouts a hundred

million years ago," Tracy grumbled.

"But they're really neat," said Julie. "Let's get them." She darted from room to room, collecting things to hang on the tree—a string of bells, a pincushion heart, Tracy's colorful god's eyes.

"Tracy, why don't you get the popcorn popping on the stove, and I'll put on some Christmas music," Mom said.

"All the records are at Dad's, too," said Tracy.

"Then how about your transistor radio?" Mom suggested. "I'm sure we can find a station that plays Christmas music."

Soon Mom was humming "Deck the Halls" and even Tracy got into the spirit, stringing the popcorn. Julie folded origami cranes, and Tracy attached thread for hanging. Then Julie and Mom got busy with construction paper and scissors, making a paper chain that snaked across the coffee table, over the beanbag chair, and out into the hall. Mom even showed them how to melt crayons in wax paper with the iron to make ornaments that looked like stained glass.

Finally Mom let out a yawn and ran her fingers through her hair. "We don't have to finish it all tonight, you know," she said.

"Are you kidding?" said Julie. "This is better than Santa's workshop!"

Mom smiled. "Well, it's past eleven—I think Santa's workshop is closed for the evening."

On Christmas Eve, while Mom closed the shop, Tracy made tacos and Julie melted chocolate in a pan for her favorite dessert—chocolate fondue. As soon as Tracy had dipped the last strawberry into the gooey mixture, Julie started to pass out gifts from under the tree.

"I made all my presents," she said, handing a box to Tracy. "Hope you like this."

Tracy ripped off the wrapping paper. Inside was a denim cover for her tennis racket sewn from an old pair of jeans and decorated with a patchwork daisy.

"You made this?" said Tracy, her face lighting up. "Groovy! Thanks, Jules."

After opening presents, they sat quietly in the half-dark by the glow of the fireplace. Julie gazed at the flickering blue flames licking the logs. She longed to be filled with the spirit of Christmas, but instead of feeling joyous, she felt strangely hollow.

"It doesn't feel like Christmas Eve," she said quietly.

Mom reached over and brushed back Julie's hair. "We had a long day," Mom said. "Why don't we all head to bed. Dad'll be here first thing in the morning."

Julie looked at her small pile of gifts—the knitting kit from Tracy, the macramé belt and embroidered peasant shirt from Mom. Something was missing, and it wasn't presents.

"I miss Grandma and Grandpa, and driving up to the farm on Christmas Eve, and going caroling . . ." Julie let out a shaky sigh. She didn't add that she missed having Dad there, too.

"I know," Mom said in a thin voice, rubbing her forehead. "Believe me, I'd love nothing more than being with both of you at Grandma and Grandpa's for Christmas. But we have to be fair to Dad, too, and just accept that—"

"—'things are different this year,'" Tracy mimicked.

Mom shot her a sharp look. "Bedtime," she said again.

"Hey!" said Julie. "You almost spit toothpaste on me." The two girls leaned over the sink, brushing their teeth.

"Well, I'm mad enough to spit," said Tracy, putting the cap back onto the toothpaste tube with an extra-hard twist. "I don't care what Mom says. I'm not going to Dad's."

"But you have to come. Besides, Mom's going to Grandma and Grandpa's in Santa Rosa. You can't just stay here all by yourself."

"I don't care. I'm not going, and they can't make me."

Climbing into bed, Julie hunkered down under the covers. But the warm quilt was no comfort tonight. Julie kicked at the twisted covers. The hall clock chimed midnight, but she couldn't get Tracy's words out of her mind.

Padding barefoot down the hall to Tracy's room, she stood in the doorway a moment before asking softly, "Tracy? You asleep?"

"Yes," said Tracy.

"Can I come in?"

"Mm-hmm," Tracy grunted. Julie took that as a yes.

"I can't sleep," said Julie.

"What's wrong?" asked Tracy, lifting up the comforter and scooting over to make a space for her sister. Julie slid into the warm bed and propped her head up on one elbow.

"Tracy," Julie started, "you just have to come to Dad's tomorrow. It won't be Christmas without you."

Tracy sighed. "C'mon, Jules. You go to Dad's lots of weekends without me. It'll be fine."

"This is different," said Julie. "It's already going to be hard enough without Mom there. But it'll be twice as bad without you."

"I'm not going to get any more beauty sleep until we talk about this, am I?" Tracy asked. Julie shook her head. Tracy propped up her pillows and leaned against the back of the bed. "This has nothing to do with you, Jules. I want us to be together, too. But everything's changed with the divorce. All my friends are here now. There's nothing for me at Dad's anymore."

"There's Dad! What about him?" Julie asked, tears stinging the corners of her eyes.

"Well, if Dad misses me, then it's his fault for getting divorced. If he didn't want to be apart from us, then how come we had to move out?"

Julie squeezed her eyes shut against the slow, leaking tears. "It'll be so lonely with just me and Dad."

Tracy wiped Julie's cheek with the soft flannel of her pajama sleeve. "Don't cry, Jules. C'mon. If it means this much to you, I'll come with you to Dad's tomorrow, for Christmas."

"Really?" Julie looked up through her tears.

"Yes," said Tracy, pulling the comforter up snug under Julie's chin. "Okay? Merry Christmas. Now, please let me get some sleep."

Julie turned onto her side, snuggling next to her sister. "Merry Christmas," she whispered.

Problems and Puzzles

❀ CHAPTER 13 ❀

Saying good-bye to Mom on Christmas morning was even harder than Julie had imagined. She waved through the back window all the way down Redbud Street until Dad rounded the corner onto Haight Street. Finally, she turned and faced forward. She missed Mom already, but she was determined to make this a merry Christmas anyway.

Twinkling lights twined around lampposts up and down Haight Street, and psychedelic wreaths adorned the front doors of shops, lifting her spirits. Julie pointed out the funny wreaths to Tracy. But Tracy just kept turning the radio dial back and forth.

"Find some Christmas carols," said Julie. "We can sing along."

"We don't need the radio," said Dad, breaking

into a verse of "Rudolph the Red-Nosed Reindeer." Julie joined in wholeheartedly.

"Oh brother," Tracy groaned.

As they turned onto their old street in North Beach, Julie hugged herself in anticipation. She pictured the Christmas candles glowing in the windows of their old house, the front door wrapped in foil like a giant gift, the mountain of presents tucked under the sparkling tree. But when she dashed up the steps to the house, no candles glowed in the windows and only the plain, dull door greeted her, stiff and wooden. Then she realized that it was Mom who always wrapped the door.

"Dad, where are the candles?" Julie asked.

"And where's the tree?" Tracy asked, pointing to the bare spot in the living room.

"Hold your horses," said Dad. "Don't worry. It's in the den this year."

Julie made her way through the house, feeling like a visiting stranger. In the den, a small three-foot tree sat on the corner end table. It had a few blinking lights, a handful of ornaments, and some tinsel.

"That's it?" asked Tracy.

"Fake?" Julie couldn't help exclaiming. "You got us

a fake tree?" She touched one of the plastic branches. "It doesn't even smell like Christmas!"

"C'mon, it's not so bad, is it? Think of all the work we saved, not having to mess with all those needles that get into the carpet."

Julie collapsed into a chair, trying to swallow her disappointment. She picked at a tiny hole in her corduroys. The rip just grew larger.

"We've got cookies," said Dad, sounding a little too jolly. "Homemade! Why don't I get us all cookies and milk, and then we can start opening presents."

Julie jumped up and ran outside to the hutch to get Nutmeg. She came back holding her rabbit close, stroking Nutmeg's fluffy coat and floppy ears. Tracy sat stiffly on a footstool, gazing out the window with her back to the blinking tree.

"C'mon, Tracy. I'm disappointed too," Julie whispered. "But Dad's trying really hard. He baked cookies and everything."

Tracy shrugged. "Big deal. It's not like we're five years old, and cookies and milk will make everything better."

"It's Dad's first Christmas without Mom, too, you

know," said Julie. "Can't you just try and make the best of it?"

"Shh. Here he comes," Tracy mouthed.

"Here we are!" said Dad, sporting a red Santa hat with white fur trim. "Take your pick." He held out a tin with layers of sugar-dusted Christmas cookies. "We have stars, trees, snowmen, you name it."

"These look great, Dad! I didn't know you knew how to bake cookies," said Julie.

"Actually," said Dad, chuckling, "Mrs. Martinelli next door brought them over this morning. Okay, girls, who wants to open the first present?"

"Me!" said Julie as Dad tossed her a shiny red box wrapped with a big bow.

In no time, the room was littered with Christmas wrappings. Nutmeg scampered around the den, burrowing under piles of wrapping paper. Julie bent over the pages of a new Nancy Drew mystery from Dad called *The Secret of the Forgotten City.*

"Thanks, Dad," said Julie. "This is the new one! I can't wait to read it."

Tracy reached over and stuck a tangled clump of stray tinsel on top of Julie's head. "And I can't wait till you see yourself in the mirror!" Tracy said, pointing to Julie's hair.

Julie grinned. She didn't care how silly she looked—Tracy was actually smiling for the first time that morning.

Tracy tore off the wrapping from her last present and let out a whoop. "Dad! I can't believe it—a princess phone! This is exactly what I wanted. Far out!" She held up a bubble-gum-pink telephone. "And it even has a light-up dial. How did you know, Dad?"

Dad smiled. "Your mom told me how much you wanted one."

"Yeah, because at home, she's always scolding me for stretching the phone cord down the hall to my room. Now I'll be able to call my friends on my very own phone," Tracy exclaimed.

"Can I run across the street and show Ivy my new charm bracelet?" Julie asked Dad.

"You'll have plenty of time for Ivy later," said Dad. "You'll be here a whole week. But today is our day to be together as a family."

"I know," said Julie, "let's play one of my new board games. How about Clue?"

"Sure, that's a great idea!" said Dad.

"Do I have to play?" Tracy asked.

"We could watch a Christmas program," said Dad. "I bet *The Grinch* is on today."

"Or *A Charlie Brown Christmas,*" said Julie.

"Cartoons? I'm in high school now," Tracy grumbled.

Julie sighed. No matter what they suggested, it wouldn't be right. Why did Tracy have to be in one of her teenage moods on Christmas? "Well, what's something you want to do, Tracy?" Julie asked.

"You guys go ahead and play a game," Tracy said with a weak smile. "I'll just listen to the radio and read my new paperback."

Julie looked at Dad and shrugged. "Well, okay," said Dad. "Maybe just one game. Later we'll think of something that will be fun for all of us."

"I call Mrs. Peacock!" said Julie, setting up the Clue game.

Tracy curled up in the overstuffed chair by the window, put the earpiece in her ear, and fiddled with the dial on her transistor.

Julie tried keeping her mind on Clue, but she couldn't help wondering why Tracy wouldn't play a game with them. Was she mad that Julie had talked her into coming to Dad's for Christmas?

After the second game, Dad rubbed his hands together and asked, "Anyone else getting chilly in here? Who wants to help build a fire?"

"Me!" said Julie. Tracy looked up but didn't budge from her comfy chair.

"Julie, grab some old newspapers, okay?"

Julie crumpled newspaper, tossing it in with the kindling. "Hey, look at this," she said, pointing to an ad in the paper. "They have a Nutcracker Tea at this fancy hotel for Christmas."

"The Fairmont Hotel," said Dad, reading over her shoulder. "That's in Nob Hill. It has some of the best views in the city."

Maybe this would help lift Tracy's spirits, Julie thought. *Who wouldn't like dressing up and spending Christmas afternoon at a fancy hotel?* A small fizz of excitement bubbled up inside her. She'd been feeling bad about forcing Tracy to come, but this would make up for it.

"Dad? Could we go to the Nutcracker Tea? We could ride a cable car. They're all decorated for the holidays. One even has a Christmas tree on top!"

"Sounds good to me," said Dad. "This looks like something we'd all enjoy."

White lights twinkled like stars along the entrance to the Fairmont. Julie felt like a princess on her way to the palace as she stepped off the red-carpet walkway and into a grand room filled with gold-veined pillars, a marble floor, and an ornate gilded ceiling.

"Wow," said Julie, twirling around. "I've never seen such a fancy place." She was glad she'd packed her best outfit, a purple paisley dress, and pleased to have such a pretty place to wear it. Even Tracy seemed impressed with all the finery.

Giant spruce trees rimmed the main lobby. Julie, Tracy, and Dad made their way slowly around the room, stopping to admire each tree. The first was hung with Russian nesting dolls of all sizes. The next was lit with Chinese lanterns and silk fans.

"Ivy would love this Chinese tree," said Julie. "And look at this one with toy nutcrackers."

"This one has sugarplum fairies," said Tracy. "They're so pretty."

"I get it!" said Julie. "Each tree is part of the Nutcracker story—like the ballet we went to last year. Remember?" Tracy nodded, her eyes flickering with wonder. Dad beamed.

When they were finished gazing at the trees, Dad ushered them into the hotel restaurant. They sat at a table beneath a glass-domed rotunda, with plush velvet seats and crystal water glasses. Even the napkins were folded into fancy swans.

"Do we have to drink tea?" asked Tracy.

"Can we order hot chocolate?" asked Julie.

"Three hot chocolates, coming right up," said Dad. The hot chocolate was served in delicate china cups, heaped with mountains of whipped cream.

"Look, the stirrer is a candy cane!" said Julie.

"This calls for a toast," Dad said, raising his cup. "Here's to being together for Christmas!" Julie raised her cup, too, clinking it with Dad's. Tracy just sat, stirring her hot chocolate into a whirlpool.

Dad waited awkwardly, his cup still half lifted in the air.

"C'mon, Tracy," Julie urged. "Clink your teacup!"

Tracy stared at the table. "I promised I'd come for

Christmas, but one day together doesn't magically make us a family again."

"We *are* a family, honey," Dad said gently.

Julie sucked in a breath. "Tracy, you act like Dad divorced *us!*"

"Well, it feels like he divorced me," Tracy said, her voice starting to wobble. "You don't even know me any-more, Dad. Ever since we had to move out, it's like you don't even care about me."

"Tracy, honey, you know that's not true." Dad reached out to tenderly squeeze Tracy's hand. She pulled it back, as if she'd been stung.

"You don't understand me at all!" Tracy said, chok-ing back tears as she slid out of the booth, knocking over a crystal water glass.

Julie's mouth hung open. Dad stood and reached out to give Tracy a hug, but she jerked free and stormed out of the restaurant. Dad and Julie followed.

In the middle of the sidewalk, right in front of the Fairmont Hotel, Tracy covered her face with her hands, heaving with sobs. Dad put his arms around her shoulders, and this time she didn't pull away.

As soon as they got home, Tracy made a beeline for her room.

Dad stopped her on the stairs. "Tracy, I know you're upset, but I just want to say one thing. I love you and want to be part of your life. But you have to let me. So when you're ready, I'll be right here. I'll always be here for you."

Tracy turned and headed back up the stairs without a word. Julie started after her. But Dad caught her up in a hug.

"Let her go, honey," Dad said. "She just needs a little time."

"But I don't understand. One minute everything's fine, and the next she's crying and running out of the restaurant."

"I know, honey. She's just hurting. Tracy and I have been apart since the divorce, and we need to find a way back to each other." Dad gave Julie a comforting squeeze and said, "Now, you and I could use a little holiday cheer. What do you say we start that new thousand-piece puzzle Santa brought?"

"Sure, Dad," said Julie, showing him a shaky smile.

Julie sorted out the edge pieces and lined them up, trying to make sense of her jumbled feelings. *If only feelings were as simple to sort out as a jigsaw puzzle,* she thought with a sigh.

The morning after Christmas, Julie woke up to birdsong in the bamboo hedges outside her window. She rubbed a swash through the fog on the window and peered across the street. Ivy's curtains were open and her cats, Won Ton and Jasmine, were sunning in the window. That meant Ivy was up. Julie threw on her corduroys and her new peasant shirt from Mom, gobbled down a muffin, left a note for Dad, and hurried across the street.

Ivy opened the front door, holding her little sister by the hand. Missy had purple jelly all over her mouth.

"Hi, Joo-hee," said Missy. At three, she still had trouble with Julie's name.

"Hi, Missy Mouse," said Julie. "Merry Christmas," she said, handing Ivy a present.

"Thanks!" said Ivy. "Come on in. Your present is

waiting for you under the tree."

Julie slipped off her shoes—a tradition at Ivy's house. She wiggled her toes into a pair of Chinese silk slippers by the front door as Won Ton and Jasmine rubbed against her ankles.

In the front room, Ivy's twelve-year-old brother, Andrew, was sprawled on the floor with his nose buried deep in a kung fu magazine.

"Hi, Andrew. Merry Christmas," said Julie.

"Uh-huh," said Andrew, not taking his eyes off the page.

"Look, Joo-hee," said Missy, holding up a miniature tea set she had gotten for Christmas. "Can we have a tea party?"

"In a little while," said Ivy. "Go ask Po Po to help you set it up."

Just hearing Ivy mention her grandmother sent a sharp pang through Julie. Were Mom and Grandma baking cookies right now, without her?

The two girls plunked down in front of the tall tree, decorated with lots of shiny colored balls and blinking lights. The gingery smell of Mrs. Ling's special pancakes wafted in from the kitchen. *Dad's house seems drab and dreary compared to Ivy's,* thought Julie.

"Your tree is so pretty," said Julie, leaning back to admire it.

"Yours must be pretty, too," said Ivy, "with all the colored lights and ornaments and tinsel."

"Not this year," said Julie.

"Really?" Ivy asked.

"It's a long story," said Julie. She told Ivy about the tears and tension of the last two days.

"Oh," said Ivy. "I thought having two Christmases would be twice as good as one."

"Think again," said Julie.

"Well, around here, it's not so great either," Ivy assured her friend. "Missy got into the new markers Andrew gave me for Christmas and decided to color the bathtub. I had to wipe down all the tile, and Andrew had to scrub around the tub with a toothbrush! It was almost as bad as when we have to clean the whole house for Chinese New Year."

Julie smiled. She knew that Ivy was just trying to make her feel better. "But you love Chinese New Year," said Julie.

"Yes, but we don't love all the cleaning." Ivy handed

Julie a tall box wrapped in snowflake paper. "Here—this'll make you feel better."

"Thanks," said Julie. She tore off the wrapping. Through the plastic window of the box, a Chinese doll with rose-red cheeks and shiny black hair smiled back at her.

"Oh, she's beautiful!" Julie whispered, carefully taking the doll out of the box and hugging her. "And this dress looks like real silk." She smoothed her hand across a turquoise dress shimmering with delicate vines and blossoms. "She's just like your doll, Li Ming."

"Her name's Yue Yan," said Ivy. "It means happy and beautiful."

"That's the perfect name for you," Julie told her doll.

Ivy raced back to her room to get her own doll. Li Ming was wearing a red silk dress. The two girls nestled the dolls in their laps while Ivy reached for her present.

"Open it," Julie urged.

Ivy's eyes sparkled when she saw the small pillow Julie had made for her. The fabric had a green-leafed ivy pattern, and in the center Julie had embroidered Ivy's name in Chinese characters. "You made this?" Ivy cried. "How did you know my name in Chinese?"

"Easy," said Julie. "I asked your mom last time I was here, and she drew the characters for me."

"Thank you!" Ivy said. "Let's go put it on my bed right now."

"Then can you show me some more Chinese writing?" Julie asked. "I like making the characters."

"Sure. Wait till you see my new calligraphy set."

Julie sat cross-legged on the floor of Ivy's room while Ivy took out a satin-lined box that held her brush-and-ink set. She showed Julie how to hold the brush with the pointed tip. "Hold it straight up and down, not like a pencil. Here, I'll show you how to write your name in Chinese." Ivy put a few drops of water in a small blue-and-white porcelain dish and swirled the ink stick in it, making a rich black ink. The girls practiced on the pages of an old phone book.

"My brush strokes look so messy!" Julie said.

"Try less ink," said Ivy. "And don't press so hard."

Julie's brush strokes were too heavy, and then too wiggly. At last, she got the two characters of her name to look the way Ivy had drawn them.

"That's good!" said Ivy.

"What does yours say?" Julie asked, pointing to Ivy's lettering.

"It means 'double happiness,'" said Ivy.

"I never knew you could letter so well in Chinese," Julie said.

"I learned it in Chinese school," Ivy told her. "We'll practice more later. Let's clean up and play with our dolls."

"Where's Tracy?" Julie asked when she got back to Dad's house. "Is she still up in her room? Do you think she'll come down?"

"She went back to Mom's today, honey," Dad told her. "Your mother's back from Santa Rosa, and Tracy just wasn't happy here."

"But I thought—"

"It's okay. I want her to feel like this is her home, too. But for now, I think it's best to give her some space. It can take time to heal the hurt from something as painful as a divorce."

Julie nodded. "I know, Dad."

For the rest of the week, Julie and Dad shot hoops

every day, sun or rain, and made dinner together every night. Besides getting to spend time with Dad, Julie loved having Ivy so close—a whole week to be right across the street from her best friend. All week, they played with their dolls, practiced Chinese calligraphy with Ivy's brush-and-ink set, and roller-skated or rode their bikes when it wasn't raining.

Before she knew it, the holiday week was over, and Julie was saying good-bye to Ivy. "I wish Christmas break would last forever," Julie said.

"I'm going to miss you," said Ivy, hugging her. "But don't worry, we'll still see each other on the weekends you're here, right?"

Julie nodded, blinking back tears. She never seemed to get used to saying good-bye to her friend. Clutching her doll to her, she ran through the light rain to Dad's house.

Good Fortune

✿ CHAPTER 14 ✿

hen Julie got back to Mom's house, it was January. Hank had already taken away the Christmas tree, and the ornaments were carefully put away. Julie tried her best to return to regular life, but she couldn't shake a hollow, unsettled feeling. As happy as she was to be back with Mom, there was still that empty place inside her, missing Dad.

After school each day, Julie read and reread her new books, put her jigsaw puzzle together for the second time, and knitted a hat and scarf for Yue Yan with her new knitting kit from Tracy. When she found herself feeling lonely, she thought of Ivy. Lucky Ivy! She had her whole family around her, plus a special celebration, Chinese New Year, to look forward to.

Two weeks passed slowly, and then it was

mid-January, and Julie was back at Dad's for the weekend. As usual, Tracy had refused to come.

Julie was just about to knock on Ivy's front door when it opened.

"Oh, hi, Mrs. Ling!" Ivy's mom usually wore a straight skirt and pretty vest, and her hair always had a just-brushed look. But today, the slender Mrs. Ling was wearing an oversized man's shirt, and her smooth black hair was hidden under a scarf.

"Julie! Come in. I was just going to shake out this rug. As you can see, we've been doing some cleaning. Only two weeks till Chinese New Year!"

Missy followed Mrs. Ling, pretending to sweep with a child-sized broom. "Out with the old and in with the new!" she said in a sing-song voice.

Ivy appeared, holding an ink brush. "Come on up to my room. You can help me make some banners."

"Have you finished cleaning all the downstairs windows?" Mrs. Ling asked.

"Almost," said Ivy.

"Windows first," said Mrs. Ling.

"I can help," Julie offered. One by one, Julie sprayed the windows in the front room, and Ivy followed close behind, wiping them clean.

"Thanks for helping," said Ivy. "Cleaning goes way faster with two."

"Yeah, but now we smell like salad," said Julie.

"It's from the vinegar in the spray bottle," said Ivy, laughing. "Let's go up to my room and I'll show you how to write the characters for *Gung Hay Fat Choy*."

"What does that mean?" asked Julie as the girls sat down at Ivy's desk.

"Good luck and good health in the new year," Ivy translated. She dipped her brush in the little dish of ink and began painting characters with a few sure, quick strokes.

Julie held her brush straight and made a Chinese character that looked a bit like an umbrella with raindrops.

"You're really getting the hang of this," said Ivy. "Hey, maybe we can make a banner to hang by the door. You should see the banners Po Po made when she wasn't much older than me. They're the ones we bring out every year for New Year's. Each one has a Chinese poem. I'm trying to copy Po Po's brush strokes." Ivy unrolled several long scrolls of paper, telling Julie what each poem said:

Springtime
New shoots grow
Taller by the spreading
Rays of the sun

Make a candle
To bring brightness
Read a book
To achieve learning

"Wow," Julie said with admiration. "Look, this Chinese character even looks like a seed pushing up out of the ground."

Ivy nodded. "The next time you come, we'll hang these up on the wall to decorate the house for Chinese New Year."

Julie couldn't wait till her next weekend at Dad's. After breakfast with Dad, she hurried over to her friend's house.

"Ivy! You got your hair cut!" cried Julie as Ivy opened the door.

"Mama says it's good fortune to cut your hair before the New Year. Cut off the old and start new. What do you think?" Ivy blew a puff of air to ruffle her new bangs.

"It's great! You look kind of like Nancy Drew with her pageboy haircut."

"Thanks," said Ivy. "Guess what? Today's the Chinatown Flower Fair! The weekend before Chinese New Year, everyone buys flowers and fruits. It's like a street carnival."

"Sounds neat," said Julie. "Are you—are you going there now?" She tried to keep the disappointment out of her voice. Ivy nodded.

Mrs. Ling stood framed in the doorway, holding Missy's hand and calling to Andrew to put his shoes on. "You're welcome to come along, Julie."

Julie's heart lifted. "Just let me go ask my dad!" she called as she raced back across the street.

On their way to Chinatown, Ivy said, "Mama, let's go the long way so that we can enter through the dragon gate." At the entrance to Chinatown, a great green gate crested with golden dragons arched over Grant Avenue. A few blocks later, Ivy pointed out her grandparents' restaurant, the Happy Panda.

As they joined the throngs of people crowding the streets, Julie's eyes grew wide with wonder. She had been to Chinatown before, but today the neighborhood was like a city unto itself, bursting with new colors, smells, and sounds. Sidewalk vendors called out in Chinese, their voices dipping and rising like songbirds as they unloaded produce from trucks. Silvery fish stared out of wooden crates labeled with Chinese characters. Racks of bright silks fluttered in the breeze, while lines of laundry flapped from second-story balconies.

The children followed Mrs. Ling up and down Stockton Street. Elbow to elbow, they threaded their way through the crowds, past cardboard boxes brimming with wrinkly vegetables and prickly fruits.

"What are all these?" asked Julie.

"Chinese cabbage, wood ear mushrooms, and bitter melon," Ivy told her, pointing at each vegetable.

"How are you ever going to eat all this?" asked Julie as Ivy's mom began to load them up with bags of food.

"Don't worry, we will," said Ivy. "Chinese New Year

lasts for fifteen days! It starts on New Year's Eve with a big family dinner at home. It ends with a feast at the Happy Panda on the night of the dragon parade—"

"—which *I'm* going to be in!" Andrew piped up. "And it's time for me to go to practice. See you later!"

"No fair," said Ivy. "We need you to help carry bags!"

"That's what you have Julie for," Andrew teased, waving and heading off toward the Chinatown Y.

"We can't forget tangerines, for good luck," Ivy told Julie. "Look for tangerines that still have stems with leaves attached. That's for friendship, and staying connected."

Julie carefully selected a tangerine with a firm stem and two green leaves. She thought about her own family, about Tracy and Dad. *If only it were that easy to stay connected.*

Soon Julie and Ivy were weighed down with pink plastic bags brimming with fruits and vegetables. Mrs. Ling piled them even higher with peach blossoms, peonies, and chrysanthemums.

"Peach blossoms are for long life, and good luck, too," Ivy said.

"We need good luck," said Julie. "Good luck carrying all this stuff home!"

Mrs. Ling paused outside a souvenir shop to talk to a woman in a red quilted jacket. Ivy and Julie set their bags down, waiting while the women spoke rapidly in Chinese.

"Hey, Ivy, is the doll shop anywhere around here?" Julie asked, looking up and down the street.

"It's just past the kite shop, a few doors down."

"Do we have time to look in the window?"

"Sure," said Ivy, glancing at her mother and the souvenir-shop lady. "They'll be talking for about a million years."

Pushing through the crowds, the girls gazed into the storefront window. "Wow," said Julie. "They have doll dresses and dollhouses and miniature furniture. Let's go inside!"

A bell jangled as they opened the door. The shop was like an attic crammed full of treasure. Jade princess dolls. Dragon tea sets, drums, and fans. Traditional Chinese papercuts. Lion masks and lanterns. Satin dresses and pajamas.

"Look," said Ivy. "They have Chinese dresses in

girls' sizes. Let's try them on."

Julie lifted a turquoise dress from the rack that looked very much like Yue Yan's dress. It felt silky-smooth to the touch. "If I had a dress this fancy, I'd ask Dad to take me back to the Fairmont Hotel. Only this time, Tracy wouldn't be there to ruin it."

Ivy selected a red dress like Li Ming's. "If I had a dress this fancy, I'd wear it for New Year's!" she said.

The girls tugged the dresses on over their clothes. They whirled and twirled in front of the long mirror. "Wish to buy?" asked the saleslady, smiling. "Not today, thank you," Ivy said politely.

The girls reluctantly hung the dresses up and hurried back outside. They ran past the kite shop, a Chinese bakery, and an herb shop. But when they got to the souvenir shop, Mrs. Ling and Missy were nowhere in sight. Even their bags were gone.

Ivy and Julie looked up and down the sidewalk, inside the souvenir shop, and across the street. "Mama!" Ivy called out, trying to see above the crowd. "Mama! Where are you?"

"It's my fault," said Julie frantically. "We shouldn't have gone inside that shop. We took too long. They could be anywhere!"

"But Mama wouldn't leave without us!" Ivy went back into the souvenir shop to ask the shopkeeper if she knew which way her mother and sister had gone. The woman replied in rapid Chinese. Ivy's face fell.

"She says they went to find us," she told Julie.

"Okay," said Julie, taking a deep breath. "Think, Ivy, if your mom was looking for us, where would she go?"

Ivy closed her eyes for a minute. "I know! She must have gone to the fortune-cookie factory. Remember? She said that was her last stop."

"Do you know how to get there?" Julie asked.

"It can't be too far from here. I know it's in a little alley, next to a barbershop. C'mon. Hurry!"

Julie and Ivy bent low and ducked through the crowds filling the sidewalk. When they turned the corner, the crowds thinned out a bit. They rushed down a few blocks, searching in every direction. Nothing looked familiar. Julie's heart quickened. She felt lost in a foreign country. Even the words people spoke were impossible to understand.

Ivy made a sharp turn into an alley where the tall backs of buildings blocked the sunlight. A cascade of overturned boxes littered the alley. Heaps of cabbage leaves were scattered every which way.

"Pee-yew! This place smells!" Julie held her nose. "Are you sure this is it?"

"No," said Ivy, her voice cracking. "I'm not sure."

"Let's try the next alley," said Julie. Somehow, as long as they kept moving, it didn't seem so scary.

As they entered the narrow alley, crumbling brick walls hemmed them in. Julie gripped Ivy's hand. An old man came up to them, pointing his cane and muttering in Chinese. "What's he saying?" Julie whispered.

"I don't know. C'mon, let's get out of here."

"Wait! Listen—what's that strange noise?" Julie asked.

"What noise?"

"That clickety-clackety sound. It sounds like rain on a tin roof."

Ivy stopped to listen. Her eyes lit up. "Those are mah-jongg tiles! It's a game Gung Gung plays." Ivy craned her neck, looking up to the second story of the old brick building. "This looks just like the place where Gung Gung plays. If he's up there, he can help us find Mama and Missy."

Taking two steps at a time, Julie followed Ivy up the iron staircase to a long open room lined with tables, where Chinese men were clustered in small groups, slapping down ivory-colored tiles that sounded like dominoes. *Clickety-clack, clickety-clack.*

"Do you see him, Ivy?" Julie asked. "Is he here?"

"Gung Gung!" Ivy called, rushing over to her grandfather. "We need your help."

As Ivy explained what had happened, Gung Gung rose from his table, spoke in Chinese to the other men, and beckoned the girls to follow him. He led them back down the iron staircase into the alley below and pointed to a brick building down the block.

A warm, sugary-sweet smell filled Julie's nose. "Yum—I smell pancakes. Or maybe French toast."

"That's the fortune-cookie factory! I smell it, too," Ivy said, sniffing the air. "Now I know where we are. Thanks, Gung Gung." Her grandfather's face crinkled into a smile as he guided the girls toward the fortune-cookie factory.

As soon as she saw Ivy's mom, Julie felt her whole body relax.

"Mama!" called Ivy, running up to hug her.

"Oh, Ivy, you girls scared me half to death!" Mrs. Ling said. "I turned around and you had disappeared. All I could think was that maybe you'd gone ahead to the cookie factory."

"I'm sorry, Mama," said Ivy, hanging her head.

"It's all my fault," said Julie. "I wanted to go inside the doll shop."

"But you're the one who heard the mah-jongg tiles," Ivy said. "If it weren't for you, we might not have found Gung Gung, and we'd still be lost."

"Well, we're all found now," said Gung Gung, putting his arms around Ivy and Julie. Missy hugged them, too. "And I have a mah-jongg game to finish." The girls waved as he turned to go.

Mrs. Ling shook her head, looking more relieved than angry. "Now, no more wandering away, please. This is not the day to get lost in Chinatown."

"We know, Mama," said Ivy as they followed the heavenly smell into the fortune-cookie factory.

Two women sat in front of machines that looked like gigantic waffle irons. Each machine poured out small circles of batter, and the women folded each circle into a half-moon fortune-cookie shape, slipping a secret fortune inside with one swift motion. The women spoke to Mrs. Ling in Chinese, and then handed each girl a fresh, warm fortune cookie.

Mrs. Ling told the girls, "Look inside for a happy new year fortune."

Ivy broke her fortune cookie in half and pulled out the small slip of paper.

"What does it say?" asked Julie between bites.

"'A new blade of grass pushes through earth to reach the sun.' How about yours?" asked Ivy.

"Mine's funny. It says, 'New beginnings are like new shoes.'"

"I don't get it," said Ivy. "How is a new beginning like a new shoe?"

Julie thought for a minute. "Well," she said, "new shoes pinch and give you blisters . . ."

"So we're going to get a lot of blisters in the new year? I'm not sure I like that fortune."

Julie looked at both fortunes as she munched the rest of her cookie. "I think," she said slowly, "they're both saying it's not always easy when you first start something new."

Gung Hay Fat Choy

✿ CHAPTER 15 ✿

"Julie," Tracy called. "Phone's for you!"

"Alley Oop? It's me, Ivy. Did you get it? Did you get my invitation to the Happy Panda for Chinese New Year?"

"Mom showed it to me as soon as I got home from school," said Julie. "We're coming for sure!"

"Mama said you've been such a big help getting ready for Chinese New Year that we could invite your whole family," Ivy bubbled.

"You mean my—my *whole* family?" Julie asked, the words sticking in her throat.

"Sure. I already took an invitation over to your dad, and he said he'd love to come. Did you know it's the Year of the Dragon?"

Julie swallowed. Thinking about Tracy and Dad together in the same room was like coming face-to-face with her *own* dragon.

"I can't wait," Ivy went on. "This'll be the best Chinese New Year ever!"

Julie hung up the phone, biting her fingernail. She wished she could share Ivy's excitement. But all she could feel was worry, and the worry turned to dread every time she pictured her whole family together in the same room. What if Tracy got upset with Dad and made another scene that would embarrass Julie in front of the Lings? She couldn't bear to think about another ruined holiday. Chinese New Year was all about good fortune and family togetherness. Right now her family didn't have much of either.

Julie bit another nail, feeling guilty. She knew she should be looking forward to the Chinese New Year celebration with Ivy and her family. *Maybe it would be simpler if I just didn't go,* she thought. But then she'd be letting Ivy down, not to mention herself.

Families sure were complicated! Julie didn't remember things being so confusing before her parents split up. She felt a nervous knot in her chest, ten times worse than when she and Ivy were lost in Chinatown.

"Julie," Mom said, coming into the kitchen, "you're

going to wear those nails down to the nub. Is something wrong? Everything okay at school?"

Julie collapsed into a chair. "School's fine, Mom. I'm just—just worried about something."

"Maybe I can help," Mom offered.

Julie looked at Mom, and in a few short minutes, she'd spilled out the whole dilemma. Just telling Mom eased the tight knot inside her.

Mom gently rubbed her back. "Oh, Julie, I'm glad you told me. I hate to see you hold so much in."

"I know, Mom, but it has to do with what happened at Dad's over Christmas, and I wasn't sure I should be talking to you about that."

"Christmas was hard for all of us this year. Just remember, if it has to do with our family, you can always come to me."

Julie nodded, her throat tight.

"As hard as it is being apart, it's not always easy being together either, is it," Mom went on. "And we're going to run into this the rest of our lives, honey. Every time there's an important event—not just Christmas, but birthdays, graduations, even weddings—we're going to face this. Maybe this Chinese New Year celebration is a chance for the four of us to practice being together."

"You think so?" asked Julie hopefully.

"I know so," said Mom, planting a kiss on her forehead.

❀

The night of the dragon parade finally arrived. Julie knocked on Ivy's front door. "Alley Oop!" said Ivy. "Gung Hay Fat Choy! Happy New Year!"

"Gung Hay Fat Choy to you, too," said Julie.

Ivy's brown eyes sparkled. "I thought you'd never get here. I'm so excited I can hardly breathe!"

"I wasn't sure what to bring to wear tonight," Julie said, holding up a brown grocery bag that had her red velvet jumper inside.

"C'mon, I want to show you something," Ivy said, pulling Julie back to her room. "Ta-da!" Ivy pointed to a red silk dress laid out on her bed.

"That's the same dress you tried on in Chinatown that day!"

"Can you believe it? It's tradition to wear new clothes for Chinese New Year, and Mama got this for me to wear."

"You're *so* lucky," said Julie. "How'd your mom know?"

Mrs. Ling poked her head into the bedroom. "Mothers know these things," she said with a twinkle.

"It helps if the lady at the shop is your friend," said Ivy, laughing. "And Mama knew this dress matched Li Ming's." Then Ivy went to her closet and pulled out a hanger. Julie gasped. It held the turquoise dress. "It's for you," said Ivy. "Try it on!"

Julie reached out to touch the dress. The silk felt as smooth as rose petals. "It's beautiful," said Julie. "You mean I can wear this tonight?"

"The dress is yours to keep," said Mrs. Ling. "To thank you for all your hard work."

"Oh," Julie said breathlessly. "Thank you so much!" She held the dress up to her neck and spun around the room, then fell on the bed next to Ivy, dizzy and laughing.

Mrs. Ling looked at her watch. "Girls, I'll take the dresses to the restaurant. It's time for us to go."

"Double happiness!" said Ivy, putting her arm around her friend.

When they got to the Happy Panda, Po Po greeted them wearing a purple quilted jacket with fancy knots for buttons. Ivy's grandmother was a tiny woman whose whole face grew rounder when she smiled. Today her salt-and-pepper hair was pinned up with red cinnabar hair sticks.

Po Po showed the girls how to set the tables, fold the napkins into fans, and fill all eight sections of the *chuen-hop*, the traditional Tray of Togetherness, with candied fruits and red melon seeds.

"Careful," warned Po Po. "Bad luck to break a dish!"

Julie and Ivy were especially careful with the gold-rimmed plates. When they were finished, each large round table glittered, a kaleidoscope of red and gold. Crystal glasses glinted in the late afternoon sun.

Julie and Ivy hurried to the back office to slip on their new dresses. Ivy gave Julie a pair of embroidered Chinese slippers to wear.

Mrs. Ling came to the door. "You girls are as pretty as a picture," she said. "Come on out and let everyone admire you!"

People began streaming into the Happy Panda—Ivy's aunts, uncles, cousins, and friends of the family—calling "Happy New Year!" and "Gung Hay Fat Choy!" Everyone brought hostess gifts for Po Po and Mrs. Ling, and, for all the children, lucky red envelopes called *lai see*.

"Each one has a dollar bill inside," Ivy explained. "Don't tell Andrew, but I played a joke on him and put Monopoly money inside one of his envelopes!" The two girls giggled, imagining the look on Andrew's face when he opened the envelope.

Soon Julie's dad arrived. He handed Mrs. Ling a box of candy. "It's marzipan in the shape of animals—my holiday favorite as a boy," he told her.

Julie grinned, delighted that Dad had known to bring a gift. Mrs. Ling accepted the box with a gracious nod. "Welcome!" she said. "Welcome to the Happy Panda."

Mr. Ling came over to shake Dad's hand. "We're so glad you could come."

"Thank you for inviting me," said Dad. "I haven't

been to a Chinese banquet like this since I was in China back in 1971."

"How did you manage that?" asked Mr. Ling, his dark eyebrows raised with curiosity. "Travel to China was banned for Americans."

"Just happened to be in the right place at the right time," Dad replied. "I had flown the U.S. table tennis team to Japan, when they unexpectedly got invited to China. I was asked to be a backup pilot on the charter flight from Tokyo to Peking."

"No kidding," said Mr. Ling, raking back his short black hair. "I remember we all had great hopes for President Nixon's Ping-Pong diplomacy."

"What's Ping-Pong diplomacy?" asked Julie.

"That's when China first renewed friendship with the United States after many years of political disagreement," Mr. Ling explained.

Ivy tugged Julie's arm. "There's your mom and sister."

Mom greeted Mrs. Ling, handing her a delicate purple orchid. "It's great to see our old neighbors," Mom said. She turned to Julie, holding her at arm's length. "Oh my—let me look at you!"

"Jules, you look fab in that Chinese dress," Tracy gushed.

"Thanks," said Julie, breathing a sigh of relief that Tracy seemed to be in a good mood.

Gung Gung tapped a chopstick against a water glass. "Honored guests," he said when everyone quieted down, "we are so happy and blessed to have you all come together with us for this special New Year's feast.

"When my father first came to this country, life wasn't easy. San Francisco seemed new and strange, so different from China and all he left behind. He had to make a fresh start. After years of hard work, he opened a restaurant, the Happy Panda. And here we are today, many years later, celebrating Chinese New Year—in America!"

Everybody clapped. Mr. Ling added, "Please, everyone, find your seat at one of the tables, and let us begin our meal. Gung Hay Fat Choy. Happy New Year to you all."

The first course was soup. Tracy peered into the bowl of murky brown broth. "What is it?" she whispered to Julie.

"Shh!" Julie whispered. "Please just eat it. It's rude

not to appreciate the food."

"I've never had authentic bird's nest soup before," Dad said.

"Bird's nest soup? You didn't tell me I'd be eating a bird's nest!" Tracy whispered back to Julie.

"Just try it, Tracy," Julie urged softly.

Tracy took a hesitant sip. "Mmm, this is actually pretty good."

"See? Trying new things isn't so bad," said Julie.

As soon as the soup bowls were cleared, trays of bright green vegetables, platters of glistening fish and chicken, and steaming bowls of rice and noodles were brought to the table.

"Long-life noodles," Po Po told the guests. "Okay to slurp. Very bad luck to cut noodles!"

"I've never seen so many colorful plates of food!" Mom said.

"Smells delicious, too," said Dad.

For a few minutes, all Julie could hear was the clicking of chopsticks. Dad kept dropping a dumpling onto his plate. Julie hoped none of the Lings had seen.

"No matter how many times I've tried eating with chopsticks, I still can't quite get the hang of it," Dad said.

"Try keeping the bottom one still, and just move the top one," Tracy suggested, turning toward Dad for the first time that evening and clicking her own chopsticks in the air to show him how.

"Hey, that really works!" said Dad, trying it out.

When the meal was finished and everyone was sipping tea and chatting, Gung Gung announced, "Time for a story! Tonight's tale goes back to the olden days in China, when the monster Nien came down out of the mountains and scared all the villagers. This monster was not like the wise dragon Gum Lung, who protects the people and brings good fortune. Nien was ferocious and ugly and struck fear into the hearts of the people. Every New Year, people locked their doors so that Nien would not come gobble them up.

"One year, a wise old man gathered the people together and told them to bring drums and gongs and noisemakers of every kind to scare the beast away.

"The next time Nien appeared, the people were ready. They beat drums and lit firecrackers. Never before had there been such a furious noise, and the monster Nien fled back into the mountains, never to be seen again. So each year, we beat drums, clang cymbals, and light firecrackers in our parade to make sure the monster Nien never returns!"

Missy peeked out from behind her hands. "Is the scary story over, Gung Gung?"

"Yes," said Gung Gung, his face crinkling into a smile. "But the parade is about to begin."

At least Tracy didn't make a scene, Julie thought to herself. But she could still feel a lump of disappointment in her chest. The dinner was over, and other than showing him how to use chopsticks, Tracy had avoided talking to Dad. The celebration hadn't exactly brought them together.

"Tracy, can't you be nicer to Dad?" Julie whispered, looking around to make sure no one else could hear.

"What do you mean?" asked Tracy. "I didn't say anything."

"That's just the point! You didn't even try to talk to him."

"I don't know what to say to him."

"Tracy, it's *Dad.* Just be yourself—talk about anything. School, or tennis—it doesn't matter what. C'mon, give him a chance. He just wants to be part of your life. Why can't you let him?"

Tracy glanced over at Dad. He stood sipping the last of his tea, studying a painting of a lone cypress hanging on the back wall of the restaurant. "I'll try," said Tracy in a soft voice.

Up on the iron balcony above the Happy Panda, Julie and her family had a bird's-eye view of the Chinatown streets below. Throngs of people jammed the sidewalks. Bright banners fluttered outside every shop, colorful paper lanterns swayed in the night breeze, and firecrackers popped in the distance.

"What a view from up here," Dad remarked. "I don't know when I've enjoyed myself so much."

"And I don't know when I've eaten so much!" Mom joked.

Tracy leaned over to whisper in Julie's ear. "Guess what, Jules. I invited Dad to my tennis match next week."

"What did he say?" Julie asked.

"He's going to come," said Tracy.

"Didn't I tell you?" Julie smiled.

They heard a thunderous *boom, boom, boom,* and

the first drums of the parade went by. There were glittering floats, marching bands, acrobats, and stilt walkers. A blizzard of red confetti from all the fire-crackers floated through the air like snowflakes, and clouds of smoke puffed skyward. Missy clapped her hands as the lion dancers dipped and bowed inside their white-whiskered, lion-headed costumes.

"Where's Gum Lung, Po Po?" Missy asked.

"Dragon will come at the end," said Po Po. "Must be patient."

"There's Andrew!" called Ivy. "Look, I see him. Wave to Andrew, Missy."

"Dragon!" shouted Missy. "Dragon, dragon!"

Right in front of the dragon's head, Andrew whirled a red ball on a long stick. The crowds went wild as Gum Lung, the great dragon, weaved its way through the streets, dipping its head, blinking its eyes, and clacking its giant mouth. The onlookers erupted in cries and applause. Missy covered her ears.

"Gung Hay Fat Choy," Po Po said above the noise. "A new year begins."

Julie thought back to how Ivy's great-grandfather had left behind his home, his family, and everything he knew to come to America and make a fresh start. Just a few short months ago, she too had felt as if she were leaving behind everything she once knew, moving to a whole new life. She'd been filled with her own fears about the divorce, about moving, about her family splitting apart.

But now, thinking about the journey Ivy's great-grandfather had taken filled her with hope for new beginnings. Tonight, even Tracy and Dad were making a new start. This night had shown that her family could come together in celebration, and Julie was happy for that.

The firecrackers died down and lingering wisps of smoke drifted like fog out toward the bay. As the last marching band passed by below, the clanging of cymbals and banging of drums reminded Julie of Gung Gung's story—how the people in Old China had made loud noises to drive away their fears. Julie held up the noisemaker Ivy had given her and twirled it. She smiled as the echoing sound rang out into the night.

INSIDE Julie's World

When Julie was growing up, many people thought only boys should become doctors or lawyers or scientists or athletes. They thought sports, especially team sports like basketball, should be only for boys. Some schools didn't even have gym classes for girls.

But these views were beginning to change. The law known as the Education Amendments of 1972 included a section forbidding sex discrimination at schools that received money from the federal government—which included nearly every school in the country, from elementary to college. This section became known as Title Nine (often written Title IX).

At first, schools didn't realize how many changes Title Nine would require. But soon they realized that the new law meant they had to provide athletic teams for girls—or else let girls play on the boys' teams.

Sports wasn't the only arena in which attitudes about girls and women were changing. By the 1970s, girls were going on to college and graduate school in record numbers. As Title Nine opened more educational opportunities to females, more women became lawyers, doctors, businesswomen, and scientists—jobs that traditionally had been occupied by men. Many women simply wanted the satisfaction of doing respected, well-paid work. Others worked because they had to. In many families like Julie's, where the parents had divorced, women had to go out and earn an income, often for the first time.

Before the 1970s, divorce was rare. Since women had limited opportunities for work outside the home, leaving a marriage often meant financial hardship. Besides, as Julie knew, getting divorced carried *stigma,* or a strong sense of public shame. Parents usually felt it was best for their children if they stayed together, even when their marriage wasn't happy.

But by the mid-1970s, women had more options. Many went back to school or started a business, so they were no longer dependent on their husbands for income. When a couple found they had different ideas about how to live their lives, they sometimes chose to get divorced.

These social changes weren't easy. Americans were reeling from other major changes. They recently had watched President Richard Nixon resign over the scandal known as Watergate. Shocked that their president had tried to cover up the burglary of files from his political opponents and then had lied to the public about it, many Americans lost confidence in their government. It sometimes seemed as if all the time-honored American ideals were being turned upside down.

For Americans such profound changes—in their government, their jobs, their marriages, and even their sports—were upsetting. But other Americans, especially young people, believed that creating a fairer society, where girls and women had the same opportunities as boys and men, would improve life for all Americans.

Read more of JULIE'S stories,

available from booksellers and at *americangirl.com*

❀ *Classics* ❀

Julie's classic series, now in two volumes:

Volume 1:
The Big Break
Julie's parents' divorce means a new home, a new school, and new friends. Will Julie ever feel at home in her new life?

Volume 2:
Soaring High
As Julie begins to see that change can bring new possibilities, she sets out to make some big changes of her own!

❀ *Journey in Time* ❀

Travel back in time and spend a day with Julie!

A Brighter Tomorrow
Step back into the 1970s and help Julie win her basketball game, save a stranded sea otter, and clean up the beach! Choose your own path through this multiple-ending story.

❀ *Mysteries* ❀

More thrilling adventures with Julie!

Lost in the City
Julie's taking care of a valuable parrot—and it's disappeared.

The Silver Guitar
A guitar from a famous rock star leads Julie and T. J. into danger.

The Puzzle of the Paper Daughter
A note written in Chinese leads Julie on a search for a long-lost doll.

The Tangled Web
Julie meets a new friend who isn't who she seems to be.

Parents, request a FREE catalogue at **americangirl.com/catalogue.**
Sign up at **americangirl.com/email** to receive the latest news and exclusive offers.

A Sneak Peek at

Soaring High

A Julie Classic

Volume 2

Julie's adventures continue in the second volume of her classic stories.

hat's that noise?" Julie asked, looking around.

"That's me slurping my snow cone," said Ivy.

"No, I mean that little squeak. Hear it?" Both girls craned their necks toward the grove of trees behind their bench.

"There—look," said Julie, jumping up. "I saw something move under that pink bush." The girls stood as still as statues. They did not hear a peep.

"Maybe we scared it," said Julie.

Weep, weep.

Julie looked at Ivy. Ivy looked at Julie. Their eyes grew wide. "There it is again," Julie whispered.

"I heard it, too," Ivy said.

"Sounds like a baby bird," said Julie. The girls peered under the azalea bush. Julie blinked. A pair of round yellow eyes blinked back at her.

"A baby owl!" she whispered. It was no bigger than a tennis ball, with pointy ear tufts and a sharp hooked beak. It was covered with downy gray fuzz as soft as dandelion fluff.

"Where's your mama?" Ivy asked.

"Maybe it's hurt," said Julie. "It must have fallen out of a nest. It's too young to fly." She peered up at the treetops, looking for a nest. "I don't see anything that looks like a nest."

"Even if we did find a nest, how would we get the baby back up into it?" Ivy asked. "And I don't hear a mama owl calling."

"All I hear are those noisy crows," said Julie, glancing at the black birds circling overhead. "They might come after it. We have to save it."

"Can't the mama owl come save it?" Ivy asked.

"What if it's lost? We can't just leave it here—a cat or a dog or a raccoon could find it." Julie untied her sweatshirt from around her waist. She turned it inside out to make a soft bed and set it under the bush next to the owl. "C'mon, little one," she coaxed. "Hop into my sweatshirt and we'll take you home."

The baby bird didn't move.

"Something's wrong with it," said Ivy.

Cupping her hand under the baby owl, Julie lifted it into the soft sweatshirt and eased it out from under the bush. The girls stood a moment, in awe of the small creature.

"Don't be scared," Julie whispered. "We'll take care of you." Carefully, she settled the bird in the basket on the front of her bike. The baby owl nestled down into the folds, as if it were being tucked into bed.

"Aw, he's sooooo cute!" said Ivy. "Look at all that soft, fluffy fuzz."

"Let's get you home, fuzz face," Julie cooed. She hopped on her bike and was just about to push off when she froze. "Wait a minute. We can't take it to my apartment. There's no pets allowed. You'll have to take it home to your house."

"I can't," said Ivy. "We have two cats, remember? The bird would last about two seconds around Jasmine and Won Ton."

"And I can't take it to Dad's house, since I'm only there on weekends, and he's away a lot." Julie twisted the hem of her shirt, thinking.

Ivy grabbed Julie's arm and pointed. "Look, there's that nice lady who told us about the butterflies. Maybe she knows about birds, too."

"Good idea," said Julie. They wheeled their bikes across the grass to the lady, who was bent over sniffing a bright red azalea.

"Excuse me," said Julie.

The woman looked up. "Oh, hello again, girls."

"We found a baby owl," said Julie, parting the folds of her sweatshirt to show the lady. "We heard it crying. We couldn't find its mother or see a nest and we thought we shouldn't leave it there all alone, but we don't know what to do."

"Looks to me like you've found a baby screech owl. They don't build nests—they live in holes in trees."

"No wonder we couldn't see any nest," said Ivy.

"Poor thing's trembling," said the woman. "It must have fallen out of a tree."

"What should we do?" Julie asked.

"It needs help right away," the lady said. "Do you girls know where the Randall Museum is? It's not far from the park. They have a rescue center there. They can take care of injured wild animals."

"It's just a few blocks from my house," said Julie. "I've passed by there lots of times."

"I'm sure they'll know what to do," said the lady.

"Thanks," Julie and Ivy called, hopping back on their bikes. Julie cooed to the little owl all the way out of the park, down Waller Street, and up the hill to the museum.

At the Randall Museum, Julie and Ivy introduced themselves to a young woman with long brown hair who was wearing hiking boots, khaki pants, and a college sweatshirt. "Hi, I'm Robin Young," she said. "Let's see what you've got there."

Julie held out the sweatshirt nest. She and Ivy told Robin all about finding the baby owl.

"Let's take a look at this little guy." Robin set the bundle down on a table in the workroom. "Looks like a baby screech owl, probably only a week or two old."

"Do you think it's going to be okay?" asked Julie.

"You did the right thing to keep it warm and safe. Most of the time it's best to leave wild creatures alone, but in this case, there's no way this little guy would have made it through the night in the park."

Pulling on gloves, she gently turned the baby owl onto its back. The owl's head was twitching, and its eyes blinked nonstop.

"Is it scared?" Julie asked.

"Probably." Robin frowned. "Has it been blinking and twitching like this since you found it?"

"Yes," Julie said.

"That's not a good sign," said Robin. "Rapid blinking and head twitching can mean that the bird's been poisoned."

"Who would poison a baby bird?" asked Ivy.

"Nobody poisoned it on purpose. Most likely, it ate something containing pesticides, like DDT."

"What's DDT?" Julie asked.

"A chemical," Robin explained. "Farmers used to spray it on their fields and orchards so that insects wouldn't eat all their crops. Then birds swallowed it when they ate the leaves or insects. A law was passed to stop the use of DDT a few years ago, but we still see the effects of it moving up the food chain."

"Do you think you can save the owl?" Julie asked.

"We'll know in the next forty-eight hours," said Robin. "For now, I'll get out a heating pad to keep it nice and warm, give it water every fifteen minutes, and see if I can get the little guy to eat a mealworm."

"Can I come back and visit him?" Julie asked.

"Sure, any time," said Robin. "I'm a graduate student at Berkeley, but I'm here most days when I'm not in class."

"Thanks," said Julie. "I'll be back tomorrow."

About the Author

MEGAN MCDONALD grew up in a house full of books and sisters—four sisters, who inspire many of the stories she writes. She has loved to write since she was ten, when she got her first story published in her school newspaper. Megan vividly remembers growing up in the 1970s, from making apple-seed bracelets to learning the metric system. San Francisco is close to home for Megan, who lives with her husband in Sebastopol, California, where she writes the Judy Moody series and many other books for young people.